WORKS OF G. W. HENRY.

30,000 SOLD.

16,000 MORE NOW BINDING.

ACTIVE AGENTS WANTED!

Never was such a thing known since the flood. Four handsomely bound books, containing about 1500 pages, mostly 12 mo., with Steel Engravings, retailed in sets at $1,50 for the four books, with a handsome discount to Agents. See Recommendations.

BOOK BINDING.

The subscriber being associated with

J. G. K. TRUAIR & CO.,

PRINTERS AND STEREOTYPE FOUNDERS

AT SYRACUSE,

is fully prepared, with Binder's Tools, Book Ornaments and accomplished workmen, to take any book from the manuscript,

STEREOTYPE, PRINT AND BIND,

Right, Tight, Neat, Cheap and Quick.

PERIODICALS BOUND AND OLD BOOKS REPAIRED.

Periodicals sent, will be returned without charge of transportation, to any Express Office between Albany and Buffalo. Address

G. W. HENRY,

Oneida, Mad. Co., N. Y.

RECOMMENDATIONS.

Rev. B. T. Roberts, editor of Earnest Christian, among many other things, says: —The book entitled "Shouting in all Ages," by the Rev. G. W. Henry, will do much to arouse the slumbering energies of the church and the world.

From the Rev. B. W. Gorham, Editor of the Guide to Holiness:—The Rev. G. W. Henry's book, entitled "Shouting in all Ages of the World," is certainly a very curious book. You will laugh without unsanctified mirth,—nay, you will laugh and cry at the same time, and yet you will, perhaps, go forth from its perusal with a deeper purpose to devote your whole being to God than ever before. In short, you get it for yourself and children, and you will very likely find it soon becoming an old book from its incessant wear.

Rev. E. Paddock, Presiding Elder of Wyoming Conference, says:—Rev. G. W. Henry may safely be styled our American John Bunyan. I have been delighted and greatly profited in reading his several works, which he has given to the public.

From the Rev. A. P. Mead, of Pittston, Pa.;—No one will doubt Brother Henry's call from God to write books and preach the gospel, that have perused his works and heard him speak, like Bunyan, having lived many years in the land of Beulah.

Dr. G. F. Hibbard, speaking of our works, says:—Wit and humor and anecdote; moral reflections, good sense and religion; quaint, shrewd, often startling and new analogies abound through the work. The reader will be made better by reading it. The author's religion is sincere and earnest and evangelical.

From the Rev. J. F. Dayan, Agent of Black River Tract Society:—Trials and Triumphs, or Travels in Egypt, Twilight and Beulah, is sought for by the people, and out-sells any other book in our colporteur's basket. Like Pilgrim's Progress, all classes read it, and all love it for its honest simplicity. It soon becomes worn out, like a child's school book. His Camp Meeting Hymns are a charming selection, old and new.

G. W. Henry & Son.

TELL TALE RAG,

AND

POPULAR SINS OF THE DAY.

In this Book a Cotton Rag is made, as it were, a living oracle, giving its own history whilst serving as raiment on twelve different Masters, relating each one of their secret, besetting and popular sins, from the time it was planted in the cotton fields of South Carolina, until it became a portion of the body of a glorified saint in Heaven.

BY G. W. HENRY,

Author of Trials and Triumphs in the Life of G. W. Henry; Wedlock and Padlock, Temporal and Spiritual; Battles and Shoutings of the Victors in all ages of the Church; Songs of the Redeemed, &c., &c.

VOL. I.

ONEIDA, MADISON CO., N. Y.:
PUBLISHED AND BOUND BY THE AUTHOR.
1861.

J. G. K. TRUAIR & CO., STEREOTYPERS & PRINTERS, SYRACUSE, N. Y.

CONTENTS OF FIRST VOLUME.

APOLOGETIC REASONS.

It is customary for authors to write what the "Fathers" called an "Apology," which, in brief, means a reason for their putting of pen to paper. The *thinker out* of "Tell Tale Rag," has many reasons, but as one, like the Rod of Moses, will successfully swallow all, one must suffice. We solemnly believe that the God of all grace has called us to this work; and for many months we have travailed in spiritual birth, being burdened and impelled by the spirit to write the tale contained in this book.

And now, unto Him, who hath converted us by his grace, washed us and made us clean, and preserved us unblamable in holiness of sixteen happy years in the land of Beulah, unto Him and to the service of our Lord and Master Jesus Christ, do we solemnly consecrate this our humble offering, and may the Holy-Ghost teach us all things, and bring all things to our remembrance that our Heavenly Father wishes us to write. Amen. Hallelujah.

G. W. HENRY,

April 30th, 1861. *Oneida, Madison Co. N. Y.*

INTRODUCTION TO FIRST VOLUME.

TELL TALE RAG
AND
'POPULAR SINS OF THE DAY.

This is a Twelve Mo. Book, of about two hundred pages, with Steel Engraving of the author and son, richly spiced with anecdotes and illustrations. Bound in two volumes, at 50 cents each. Any one enclosing 50 cents in postage stamps, shall have the first volume sent them by mail to any Post Office in the United States, free of postage; or the two volumes for $1,00, or any other work of the author at the same rate.

In this work the Rag is made a living oracle, as if it were relating its own history; tattling every thing it saw and heard, and exposing the iniquities and fashionable sins of its several owners, while clothing their persons, by night and by day. Commencing its autobiography where it was planted in the Cotton Fields of South Carolina, by Uncle Sam and Aunt Dinah, pious slaves on the plantation, who were made the hero and heroine of these volumes; about the same as Uncle Tom and Aunt Chloe were represented in the Log Cabin.

The cotton rag after passing through the hands of seven different masters, or owners, next finds a lodging at the Paper Mill, where a general assembly of fellow rags in tribulation have been gathered from the four quarters of the earth.

and where several rag conventions will be held. And it is from this place that Tell Tale Rag dictates to the publisher and binders of this work. Relating the things which he saw and heard in the past, unto his present position; and from thence onward, relating the things that happened to his four subsequent masters, whose hands he perchanced to fall into. Being reduced three times to dust, strange to tell, he at last becomes a part of a body of a glorified saint in heaven, where he recognizes Uncle Sam and Aunt Dinah, who planted and cultivated him in South Carolina, with many other saints.

Tell Tale Rag's first master was a Southern slave holder. On the first fifty pages of this work are exposed the legalized, popular and fashionable sins of the slave-holding system, both nationally and individually.

The second master whose hands Tell Tale Rag falls into is a Northern slave-holder, in the city of New York, who is a kind of a cotton professor of religion, who, by virtue of a chattel mortgage, sells at auction all the negroes, hogs, horses and cotton, on the plantation of his first master. In him Tell Tale shows how the interest of this iniquity is interwoven as a web with the North and South, both in Church and State; which takes up about twenty pages of the book.

The third master of Tell Tale was a cotton manufacturer at the Pemberton Mills, Mass. By him Tell Tale exposes many fashionable sins of the day, by mixing religion with the world, spiritual and political adultery. This master was a fusionist, a compromiser, as he would card together cotton and wool, give it a beautiful color; weave it into a web, then swear it off upon his customers as all wool. In this way Tell Tale says many church members are fusing and compromising with the world, the flesh and the Devil, expecting to pass current into Heaven, as pure Anglo Saxon.

The fourth master of Tell Tale was a retail merchant in Central New York, who was also an Oddfellow and Freemason. By this time Tell Tale is made into a cotton web, and is laid on a conspicuous place over the counter, where he takes notes in short-hand of the popular and fashionable lying, which is so prolific between merchant and customer, as the process of jewing down is going on among all traders of the day. Tell Tale also then exposes many fashionable, silent, deceptive falsehoods made up of perrywigs, dye stuffs, paints, glas eyes, &c. After that he takes up the subject of secret societies. On this subject several other rags in the scavenger's bag relate their experience while warming the backs of several individuals of the fraternity, and after listening to ten or fifteen pages of cotton field theology from Uncle Sam and Aunt Dinah in their own language, on the subject of the forbidden fruit.

Tell Tale is then sold to his fifth master, who was a blind man, who also entered into contract to publish the history of Tell Tale Rag. Tell Tale was now soon warming and comforting the limbs and body of his new master, where he takes up about sixty pages of the volume, in dissecting his new master, joint after joint, exposing the plague spots of sin on his soul and body, dragging into day light many abominable and fashionsble sins his new master was guilty of while he was dashing in the world, previous to his natural blindness and religious experience. Speaking also of several high peaks of worldly glory, from whence his master was several times tumbled down to the mud-sills of degradation, where grace at last gets her arms around him, and, step by step, bears him along until she sets him down in the land of Bullah.

INTRODUCTION TO SECOND VOLUME.

The subject of the second volume of Tell Tale Rag and Popular Sins of the Day, which is now partially written, and expects to be ready for sale about the first of August, will be the history from the sixth to the twelfth master.

The sixth master will comprise a short history of happy John, showing how deep rum had sunk him into the slough of degradation and misery, and to what heights grace has elevated him, to purity, holiness and unfading honors.

The seventh master whose hands Tell Tale now falls into, was a scavenger, whose occupation was to gather up rags that were scattered in the streets of the city, and stow them into his bag; one of which happened to be nothing less than the author of Tell Tale Rag, who had been worn out in the service of his blind and fifth master; then torn into rags and served his sixth master as a sticking plaster on his gangrened shins; from thence to the gutter, where he was drawn forth by his seventh master, the scavenger. Several interesting anecdotes are related by the rags, while assembled at Rag Bag Hall, until they were purchased by a paper maker, who becomes the eight master of Tell Tale; and from whence he dictates this volume.

At this general assembly of rags, several conventions will be called, where the fashionable and popular sins of the day will be freely discussed; such as Sabbath breaking, hop growing for distilleries, tobacco chewing and smoking, extravagant wardrobe, jewelry, and other outward adornings, buying and selling pews, praising God by machinery, together with other kindred topics, which will be freely discussed, for and against, by members of the rag convention from all parts of the world; and when the convention is adjourned they will then be ground to pulp and made into paper, assorted according to their different family relations; spiritualizing in this last process, a work of purification and holiness, until Tell Tale is made into a pure white sheet, without spot or wrinkle; when he soon exchanges owners and becomes the property of the American Bible Society, in the city of New York, whose principal Agent becomes his ninth master, and very soon Tell Tale finds himself a beautiful bound family Bible, on whose pure leaves the impress of all the exceeding great and precious promises are printed, in the Chinese language.

About this time a dashing young lady is soundly converted to God, and exchanges her jewelry for the honorable Tell Tale Rag, personated in Jehovah's own book.

His next and tenth master was a Missionary, who carried him with safety over the rolling tide, and entered with him through a breach in the Chinese wall, which was made exclusively for a gospel gate, with Britton's Artillery.

Tell Tale is now presented by the Missionary in the name of Jesus Christ to a Heathen Father, who becomes his eleventh master; and as he begins to read the sacred pages, the great eye-opener that walked in disguise with the two disciples, on their way to Emmaus, stood, says Tell Tale, unseen by my master, at his elbow, and opened unto him the sacred truth on the leaves of this spiritual tree, which he held in his lap, a healing balm for all nations; and as he read he believed, and was saved. Then he pressed the water of life to the thirsty lips of his wife and children, and very soon, says Tell Tale, my master's house became a house of prayer

The leaven being well hid in the meal, and in short, a great revival of religion ensued, until the promises on Tell Tale became obliterated, both by penitent and joyous tears, until it was literally worn out and new Bibles taking its place; Tell Tale was then cast into the garden, where soon it was reduced to the same dust from whence it originated in the cotton fields. A hill of corn was planted in the soil made fertile by the death and decay of Tell Tale, and by its vegetating powers soon transformed the remains of Tell Tale into its tender blade, until it became the full ripe corn in the ear. The corn was then made into bread, which was eaten by a Chinese Missionary; and now Tell Tale Rag has become the outer man, flesh and blood of one of God's heralds; and when his warfare was ended Tell Tale was encoffined, where he was the third time reduced to dust, and remains sleeping until the blast of the archangel, who will announce the coming of his twelvth master, that will in a moment transform the dust of Tell Tale into a royal mansion, an eternal habitation of the redeemed spirit of his eleventh and Missionary master.

This will be the last and eternal change of the masters of Tell Tale Rag, for he will then be satisfied as he wakes up in the likeness of his Lord and master Jesus Christ. Amen.—Hallelujah.

MY FIRST MASTER.

CHAPTER FIRST.

Dear reader, and fellow traveler, if you have read the introductory pages of this work, you can follow out the programme of the author. You have placed in your hand a key which will open every apartment in this humble edifice, from its twelve foundation stones upward to where the key stone is let down with "shoutings of grace, grace unto it."

Its topmost heights reach to the kingdom of glory, where the author desires to meet you, dear reader, and he prays that this little book may, under the blessing of God, be instrumental in bringing many souls to pardon, peace, and endless bliss. Amen, Hallelujah.—Now, as you are waiting for disclosures, I will introduce to you the veritable "Tell Tale Rag," who will show you, that "there are more things in heaven and earth, than you have dreamed of in your philosophy."

Disclosures of "Tell Tale Rag" about himself.

You have been already introduced to me under the cognomen of "Tell Tale Rag," having, as my name imports, lost my good name by, like a little child, tattling about every thing I saw or heard; and as you have already learned that I am solemnly pledged to relate to my publisher and binder the secrets of my twelve masters into whose hands I have at different times fallen, so I promise with a sanctified recklessness to drag into broad day-light many fashionable sins, and some, perhaps, which the church and the world generally are strangers to. Yes, by the help of the Lord, I will rebuke wickedness whether in the gutter of infamy, or perched upon the throne with the adulterous Herod, if I knew for a certainty that the daughter of his silk stocking paramour would triumphantly present my head to her mother as soon as I laid down my quill at the close of this volume. I will begin my narrative by speaking of my first master: He was a slave holder; his father and mother were South Carolina bloods; they could trace their pedigree to the loins of kings; from him whose sir-name was "Cotton," backward to the Herods and Pharaohs; which is, I believe, as far back as we can trace the glorious institution of slavery.

In reading their history, one is impressed that the "BLOOD ROYAL" was cut off at the Red Sea, when its waters closed over the hosts of Egypt, or certainly when the fathers of the institution had a ride on the back of a few thousand grunters which they used as barges to convey them from the land of the Gergesenes, down a steep place into the sea, where, as history tells us, they perished in the waters.

But to the world's astonishment, Pharaohs and Devils have like Canada thistles sprung up in all our fields, so that there are still many Bloods Royal on the earth, and as one writer dared to say,

> "They boast still of their Royal blood,
> Which has flowed through scoundrels since the flood."

So you may understand reader, when you see my first master, what a precious lump of porcelain, so "fearfully and wonderfully made," you are gazing upon.

At the birth of young Napoleon the first, the Emperor had cannons placed within speaking distance of each other, all through the kingdom of France, so that the moment it was announced that Maria Louisa was about ready to present to the Emperor a noble son, that moment a cannon roared out the intelligence that a child was born, and a son given to France, and in a moment, comparatively, all France roared with the news-speaking cannon in all its borders, for a new twig of nobility had made his appearance upon the earth.

Well, there was about as much fuss and noise made throughout the old plantation, when the birth of my young master was announced. The first business of the Royal family was to hunt up a fresh nurse, (it being considered a very vulgar thing for his royal mother to nurse her own offspring,) the fountains that the God of providence caused to flow, must be dried up; and the unnatural mother must sink into a degredation far below the beasts of the field, for nothing but death will prevent the streams of natural affection, even in brutes, from flowing for their offspring, the pure milk of a mother's love. This I will set down as a fashionable sin in high life, No. 1.

But here I will drop the thread of my narrative, to consider a subject which has, I believe, never been exhausted in all the debating clubs, lyceums, nor philosophic enquiries in any age since the world began:—Whether the hen which laid the eggs, or the one which hatched and scratched for them, or brooded them under her fostering wing, was the true mother of the chickens. My young master was in a similar predicament; for it so happened that Aunt Dinah, whom I have spoken of, had presented to Uncle Sam, her husband, about that time, an heir, which in the slave market, would have sold for ten dollars to one, better than my young master; but notwithstanding this, in consequence of his bearing the image of his parents, having his hair kinked most beautifully without the aid of the barber's tongs, and his outside wrapper having a different hue from the Circassian race, he, like Ishmael, the child of the bond woman, was obliged to give place to the son of the free woman. Poor Hagar! none but a fond mother can sympathize with her as she lays a whole ocean of love reduced to a little dew drop in the form of her infant—as she presses the last kiss, as she supposes, upon its pale cheek, and lays him down amid the shrubs of the wilderness, to starve to death; —this is a scene which a mother has not nerve sufficient to witness, and as she sits down at a little distance, and begins to look backward on past history, and then casts her eyes all around her and discovers nothing but death grimly staring in the form of starvation pressing with every wind-breath, and perched upon every bough. Oh God how I pity thee! Now sinking despairingly on the earth she cries out "no one on earth careth for me, or loves me, or my dear babe, neither doth any one see me."

But Hagar was roused from her desponding revery, by Him who is a present help in time of trouble. A voice from a golden pinioned angel, whispered in her solitary ear, "God seeth thee, Hagar, thy Father in Heaven has bottled every tear shed by thee, and thy darling babe;" and very soon the disconsolate mother and child were banquetting at the luxurious board of the Patriarch Abraham in the canvassed city of Hebron. But to resume my tale: I was at this time about "knee high" to Uncle Sam, in the cotton field; yet the scene is as fresh in my mind to-day, as when it happened, though I am now grown grey-headed amidst the terrible disasters, and changing scenes of my checkered life. But the scene which my eyes that day beheld was graven deeply on my youthful heart. I refer to the day when Uncle Sam and Aunt Dinah were obliged to surrender their first born, that heavenly pledge of connubial love, that golden link between angels and men, to the unfeeling keepers of the slave nursery, a kind of pig pen, to be fed on slops, or suck a bacon rind, to be fitted up for a Legree's or Haley's slave market. We have contemplated the struggle of Hagar, and of the Patriarch Abraham when the order came for the sacrifice of Isaac, but their sorrows were none in advance of those deep, soul-crushing realities which were transpiring in the hovel of Uncle Sam, and Aunt Dinah, when the order came for them to give up their first born ; piteous loves were rudely lacerated, and the angels of compassion hid their tear-bedewed eyes, covered with their wings.

Had this yielding up of their babe been at the demand of the grave worm, or been the immolation on Mount Moria, or even like Rachel's, when her children fell beneath the death-stroke of the hirelings of Herod, she could have seen their brains dashed upon the walls, and been comforted, knowing that their little spirits had gone to glory. But the reader may ask me, if these slaves are capable of the same intensity of grief, as the more talented and educated white race?— I answer that their sorrow is tenfold more sorrowful when conjugal ties are cut asunder, and parental heart strings are left to bleed on and on, and they are chafed and scourged with the sneers of scorners, and scorpion whips all their lives, with nought to ameliorate their condition, or comfort their hearts. The reason of which is, that they have nothing else on earth to love, but wife, children and friends; and their rude hovel is to them the boundary of their earthly paradise. When they fall asleep in each other's arms, on their humble couch of straws, and dream of heaven, this with them concludes the sources of earthly happiness; while the freeman, when providence takes away one comfort, when death with his keen knife severs one branch from his vine, has a thousand other things to fill his loves, cause him to forget his sorrows, and dry up his tears. Do you think, dear reader, that while this young sprig of nobility, this young cotton-head was exhausting the two precious fountains of life, which by a God-given right belonged to Aunt Dinah's own child, that he drew from her, or dried up the fountains of natural affection, or a mother's love? Oh no! Men have reared their walls, and barred their prison gates, and defied the entrance of their fellow men; but parental love will laugh at all such fortifications. Admiration will walk with its friends, as long as they please it; and then bid them adieu. Respect will keep us company, as long as we are respectful. Wealth will recognize us as long as we are wealthy; but parental love will leap every barrier, spring back every bolt, enter any gloomy cell in search of husbands, children and friends, that they may comfort them, yes, if they are found swinging by the hair on the arm of the forest oak, or suspended by the ignominious halter, still from the depths of the loving heart will issue the wail, "my son, my son Absalom, would God I had died for thee, Oh Absalom, my son, my son!"

Now think you, that these descendants of Ham, who, according to the slave code of South Carolina, had been robbed of their first born, did not love it still? even when forbidden, in person, to visit or comfort it? Alas! what fears rise in that slave mother's bosom when in the prospective she traces the footsteps of her daughter from infancy to womanhood, under the dynasty of this Cotton King, who has ever held female virtue, when encased in a sable skin, as the free plunder of white libertines; as much so as are the foxes for the blood hounds, that make the southern mountains re-echo again as at the midnight hour they pursue, and worry their defenceless prey. These tear-drenched parents look through those blinding vapors, see her become a mother of the children of fornication or forced adultery, until turning the page a scene is presented more fearfully terrific and heart rending. He who would delineate this tragedy, must pluck his quill from the Raven of perdition, and fill his ink horn with the poison of asps. What is this scene so terrific, this tragedy so awful? *It is the Slave Auction!* Horrors upon horrors! Reader, empty the basin of Lakè Erie, and gather the tear-drops which have fallen in this Pandemonium of hell for the last half century, and pour them in and you shall have a full bank! Then stand at the foot of roaring Niagara and listen to its terrible thunderings as those tears fall in immense billows, and you will have a faint idea of those crimes against humanity, perpetrated, while hopeless cries have entered the ears of the God of Sabbaoth! Look you, as fragments of these loving families are hitched to different chain-gangs of this Cotton King, and are driven to their unknown destination! Then think of a mother's love. You will then understand the Prophet's query, "can a mother forget the sucking child?" His reply implies that instances have been known, rare indeed, but still you will find them too plenty, who are like any slave-holding mistress in the sunny south. This we set down as a fashionable sin of the day, No. 2.— But I must hasten on with my rehearsal.

Our young master continued to grow up as a calf in the stall. Aunt Dinah's first born was sold to the trader in the souls and bodies of men, and driven to, where she knew not. Like Topsy, reared in brutal ignorance, who declared to Miss Ophelia, in honest simplicity, that she never was born, never had father or mother, but "spect she growed," so was this first born of my master weaned, and stalked about rejoicing in the possession of his cotton crown. Uncle Sam and Aunt Dinah were sent back to the cotton field, where they took up the hoe and began to cultivate me and my brethren. and sisters, who were planted in the same patch with myself, some of whom, by your permission, I shall introduce hereafter in the progress of my story. We were at this time like our neighbors, almost arrived to our full stature, and began to listen with great interest to the conversation of our cultivators as they pulled up the noxious weeds which sprung up at our roots, and would have choked us to death but for diligent culture. Uncle Sam was a holy man, and apt to teach, and so preaching and hoeing went on together.

CHAPTER SECOND.

I will introduce this chapter by informing my reader somewhat in relation to the whereabouts and history of this patriarch of the cotton field, Uncle Sam. He was born in Maryland, which, like her neighbor, Virginia, has been the hot-bed and nursery in furnishing slaves for the more tropical regions of the South. Uncle Sam's mother was a Christian in the full Gospel sense of the word; and she planted deeply, in the youthful furrows of his heart, the precious seed, and so watered it with a mother's tears and prayers, that she presented him a whole burnt offering to God. This seed, as I have suggested, took deep root, and in due time sprang forth "the tender blade," and it matured, "the full corn in the ear." At this time he was sold to my present slave master, and soon "took up"—as the Southern phrase is—and lived with Dinah, who also soon became with him a joint heir of the grace of life, and it is under their instructions and earnest words which fell from their lips that I am indebted for all the goodness which may be about me.

Alas! how often have they watered my roots and those of my fellows, with bitter tears, as they conversed (secretly of course) about the probable fate of their first born, and yet how often have they shed tears of joy in the anticipation of that place "where the wicked cease from troubling, and the weary are at rest." But the greatest difficulty which they encountered was to smother those repinings against Providence, which, like distant thunder, continually murmured, questioning the justice of a righteous God, who seemed to permit the hearts of his people to be wrung with anguish, and they, like David, would look at the prosperity of the wicked, until their feet had well nigh slipped. Nevertheless, there were hireling ministers, in sheep's clothing, ready with their pro-slavery chloroform every Sabbath, who would hush their feelings, temporarily, into a quietus. Sometimes Uncle Sam and Aunt Dinah made me think of my master's cow when she got choked with a potato, so that she could neither get it up or down. A ball was fastened to the end of a rod, which was, when completed, called a "probang." This was thrust down the cow's throat, and the potato rammed home to its destination.

It was so with these *slave-holding* preachers, or, if not that, *slave-holder's* preachers, who, with the "probang" of the Devil, were thrusting down garbled Scriptures into the hearts and ears of their hearers.—These so set forth the word of God in unrighteousness that the great mass of dwellers in slave-land, black and white, half believe that slavery and its kindred abominations is endorsed by the Scriptures. The ball that the master, or his hireling minister, makes use of most frequently as a religious "probang," the more effectually to silence their murmurs and indignation, is found in the ninth chapter of Genesis. A wad is made of Ham's blanket, which was withheld from covering the nakedness of his father while in a state of intoxication, and in consequence of this neglect, all of his posterity were to be the servants of servants.

This most generally relieved their choking for the time being, because both their master and preacher told them the same tale. Furthermore, it was in the Bible; therefore they must swallow it, of course, cooked up and seasoned, as it always was, to suit the occasion and circumstances If any doubts arose as to the complexion of Ham, the progenitor, this was at once settled by the very name he bore. They were then pointed to the black hams which were hanging in their master's larder, and told that they (the hams) derived their name from this recreant son of Noah. . They were further informed that the black bacon rind which their children were sucking was the very color of their faces, and that this ought forever to settle the question of their pedigree. True, this kind of theological chloroform must be administered, dose after dose, and repeated on all occasions of choking and rising rebellion But to Uncle Sam and Aunt Dinah, this was like talking philosophy to a she bear robbed of her whelps. There was a volcano down deep in the caverns of their hearts, and, in spite of Ham's blanket or the hams in the larder, there would be an eruption which, like the red-hot tears which run down the slopes of Ætna, would scald as they rolled, and plow deep furrows in the cheeks and hearts of these sable children of

Africa. Sometimes they would be almost ready to murmur against God, while at the same time they were ready to deprecate the fault of Ham for not concealing his father's shame. Yet, reason as they would, they could not reconcile the ways of God with them with His justice and mercy. Nor could they understand why they and their children should be enslaved everlastingly for that with which they had no personal connection. How a just God should punish them and their children so cruelly because Ham behaved badly, was a choker.

I recollect that upon one occasion, my master, in order to silence the murmurings of Aunt Dinah, (who, like Rachel, refused to be comforted for the loss of her first born,) came into the cotton field, and, after a stern rebuke, undertook to convince her that she never had a child for whom she should weep. He then directed her attention to an old mare, which was grazing in a field hard by, and thus questioned her:

"Don't that mare belong to me, Dinah? Did not I pay my money for her, the same as I did for you? Does the colt by her side belong to her or to me? and does not the Lord say, Dinah, that I have a right to do with my own as I please?"

She answered, "I s'pose so, massa," being compelled to utter with her lips that which her heart and common sense refused to endorse. She was compelled to take down the idea that she never had a child that she could truly call her own; but must be deprived of even the consolation of the old mare, or even the base swine, the privilege of nursing and weaning her own offspring. But there was another question which was and is a choker, which no slave-holders nor hireling priests have ever been able to ram down their own throats or those of the benighted slave. The question is this: "Why Aunt Dinah's babe should not be as precious, and as much honored and comforted by all sensible persons of every color, as the white woman's child?" Both, like the irresponsible and unborn Jacobs and Esaus, have never known good or evil, and both, dying in infancy, alike are heirs of heaven. Who has a right to institute a difference where God has made none? All the advocates of slavery on this point are as speechless as the Pharisee at the nuptial feast. I have never heard any better reason than can be illustrated by the following anecdote. It was related to me by one of my sisters, who was planted in the same field and reared under the same fostering care, and, subsequently made into Merrimac calico, was appropriated to the form of a waiting maid in the family of Mr. and Mrs. Arlington, in the State of Maine. After being worn out by this lady, she found herself close by my side in the scavenger's rag-bag.

Among many other interesting tales, she related the following:

Mr. and Mrs. Arlington were blessed with several sons and daughters, among whom was a very handsome and talented boy, by the name of Lewis. Unfortunately, Mr. A., her master, often came home rather top-heavy, or drunk. On all such occasions, without furnishing the least pretext for the action, he was sure to give the boy a flogging. When challenged for a reason for such conduct, his only reply was, that he "fancied that Lew looked like Dr. Hooker, the family physician."

Now, I defy all apologists for slavery, whether in pulpit or pew, North or South, if there is standing room for them on the plains of Sodom, to coin out a better reason, a more sufficient apology, for their heaven-daring cruelty than the one given by this disciple of Bacchus, viz: that they look like Dr. Hooker, or one of the sons of Noah.

Ham's blanket is not long enough to cover their hydra head, nor their cloven feet, when inquisition for blood is made by a sin-avenging God, and all those tears and groans which have fallen to the lot of the despised Ethiopian throughout the land of America's Southern Egypt. This was one of the tolerated and fashionable sins which my first master and mistress were steeped in, notwithstanding their royal blood and high professions of religion. And I think, with Aunt Chloe, bereaved of her husband, that, "If the Devil don't get such professors and preachers, then there is no use of having a Devil."

CHAPTER THIRD.

Patient reader, I have kept you twice as long contemplating the scenes in the cotton-field as I at first intended. In my first chapter, you were made acquainted with my slave-holding master, one of the bloods royal, whom we found while tracing the stream of oppression to its fountain head in Egypt. In the same region we will find the origin of the slave-holding system; it was a little beyond the Red Sea where we also find the "Fugitive Slave Law" first enacted, and practically illustrated. The tyrannical Pharaoh, with his forty thousand chariots, was hotly pursuing a large number of fugitive Israelites, when he was intercepted by the inventor of the underground railroad, who drew out the linch-pins from his chariot wheels, and placed this slave monarch and his marshalls in the same predicament as the swine of the Gergesenes. Upon this, the fugitives struck up a tune on their timbrels, and celebrated this water-burial by a dance upon a green on the farther side. Then you could have heard this "peon" of victory, "Sing ye gloriously; the horse and the horseman are lost in the sea." If this same insulted Author of freedom, whom these modern Pharaohs have the audacity to enroll as their friend and abettor, should give them a free lodging some where alongside of the Atlantic telegraph, I, for one, should hang no crape on the knob of my door, but would willingly allow them to go to their own place; and my oppressed brethren and sisters would leap for joy on the very soil which they have culti vated, and baptized so often with the sweat of their face, their blood and their tears.

"Amen, Hallelujah, for the Lord God Omnipotent reigneth."

We have been following up the stream of oppression to find the origin of slavery. I will now gratify your curiosity by a search for the initiative of SECESSION. This child, as many suppose, of the cotton king, born in the nineteenth century, is really a grand-child, and, for ought I know, a great grand-child; however, "further the deponent saith not." South Carolinian secession is only the out-working of a movement which dates far back of the Pharaohs; and our seceders certainly have Scripture to prove that it originated in heaven itself. The first secessionist that history gives any account of was once a bright star in the galaxy of heaven. There was also another prince by the name of Michael, who was always proclaiming liberty to the captives. He was a "Free-Soiler," one of the elect and precious, and was of the lineage of Abraham. In him was vested all power, in heaven and earth; and he had two keys which were suspended from his girdle. By virtue of these two keys there was a probability that he would be able to maintain his throne and dominions against all opposition. Consequently, Lucifer (for this was the name of the first secessionist) seceded. When he went, about one-third of the nation joined him under his piratical flag. They were not turned out of the Union, but St. Jude says that "they left their own habitation; they kept not their first estate." His Satanic Majesty, if you should ask him this day, would tell you that he left of his own accord, and that all he asks now of Michael and his abolition friends is to be left alone; and that Michael and his men must cease blowing their ram's horns around, troubling their neighbors, for they had already thrown down thousands of his best fortifications; and by their under-ground railroad he was likely to lose a good share of those whom he had taken captive at his will. This is the ancient landmark of the order of slave-holders; their secession prince and leader can trace his pedigree to, and in heaven; but since his going out of the Union, it is as low as Hell. And now that I am old and gray-headed, and reduced to a cotton rag, I am beholding the terrible fruits and results which were prophesied in my early youth by my patriarch and Christian nurse in the cotton field of my old master in South Carolina, long, long ago.

I have spoken of the two keys which hung from the golden girdle of Michael. Their possession by him was the cause of the first secession movement in heaven. One key, which is emblematical of power and authority, was to be used for the springing back of the bolt of every moral prison, and to take from his Satanic Majesty his poor slaves, and bring them on Michael's under-ground railroad from the brick yards of Pharaoh to the free soil of the spiritual Canaan. The other key upon the golden girdle was a terrible emblem of horror to this old secessionist, for he well knew that this was held in reserve to lock himself and his back-sliding votaries in the prison-house of hell, and would spring back the bolt of eternity upon them, when turned by "him that shutteth and no man openeth." Another idea has suggested itself to my mind, which was occasioned by my being gathered, with many others of my companions in tribulation, and thrown promiscuously among the rag bags in the paper mill. Being banged about with other rags, paper and strings, with now and then a stone, which was probably put in by the sellers to in:

crease the weight, I chanced to see upon a dirty piece of paper, the following anecdote:

Two gentlemen were seated in the cars. One of them, a pert lawyer from my native State, South Carolina. He was a little deaf. The other was a northern politician. While they were hotly contending and proposing, for about an hour, who should next fill the Presidential chair, a gentleman who was sitting near them, and had listened attentively to their debate, (this gentleman, I had forgotten to say, was a modern adventist.) tapped them both gently upon the shoulder, and said, "Gentlemen, Jesus Christ will be President the next four years." At this, the lawyer at once clapped his hand upon his pocket-book and drew forth a fifty dollar note, and thus addressed the disciple of adventism: "I will bet fifty dollars with you or any other man, that South Carolina don't go for him."—Whether my friend with the ear infirmity understood the name of the candidate he was betting against I know not. However, before I was ground all to a pulp by my master, the paper maker, I had the extreme satisfaction of reading on another scrap of paper the result of the Presidential election of 1860.—This stated that the keys were now hung on the girdle of Abraham, a free soil prince, and then I was glad that my adventist friend did not take the bet spoken of, for he would certainly have lost it; for no candidate who, like Abraham, endeavors to follow in the footprints of Michael, his illustrious predecessor, could have ever obtained the popular vote of my native State; at any rate, not that of my first master. Now, when I read in still later news of the secession, that the tropical star under which I grew had fallen from the galaxy of heaven, and, like Lucifer, the father of secession, had drawn about a third part of the stars, with the tail of his influence, down with him, I then thought, in my solemn meditations, as I took a review of the past, familiar though I was with the horrors of the slave code, of the striking analogy that existed between the first and the last acts of secession, and how clearly applicable was that Scripture, "Ye are of your father, the Devil, for his works ye will do;" or, in other words, what a striking resemblance exists between the secessionist, Lucifer, and his Southern children. No one can be left to doubt their legitimacy or their heirship to all their father's inheritance, unless they change their course. Truly, "there is no new thing under the sun." Another point of analogy which has forcibly impressed my mind, in the first and last secession movements, is the wonderful desire for office—the hot clamorings for glory and honor, loaves, fishes, &c. But the prospect of a continuance of high seasoned food was blasted when the father and his children beheld those envious keys on the girdle of

Michael, or the waist-tightener of our political Abraham, so they revolted and said, "give us the keys that bind the sons and daughters of Ham to our juggernaut, or give us death. Yes, death on the field of battle; we would prefer to reign in hell, to the service of this free-soil prince either in heaven above or on the earth beneath."

These are some of the national sins perpetuated under constitutions and human laws, which the higher law of Michael, the free-soil king, is now besieging and abrogating. This slave-driving Belshazzar has seen the hand-writing upon the wall, this cotton king is being weighed in the balances, the appointed Cyrus with his army is at the gate, the rich banquet, purchased by the blood of the children of the Most High, all such tables will be soon overturned, the goblet fall from the palsied hand, and the banqueters become the banquet for worms. Even so, Amen.

CHAPTER FOURTH.

Suffer me, reader, to hold you by the skirt, a little longer in the cotton fields; and be patient with me and we will soon have a ride together behind the iron horse, as he snorts and whistles on his way to my next master, who resides in New-York.

There has been one question which has been propounded at least a thousand and one times, and never perhaps satisfactorily answered, viz: "Whether my slave holding master, and slave holding, and slave apologizing preachers, do really enjoy true evangelical religion, which saves them every moment, through grace?" This has been a point of serious query to myself, and has also been the frequent theme of conversation among my fellow rags that have with me been assembled together from the four quarters of the earth, and emptied into the paper mill. Indeed we have had some jolly times together as we related to each other many ridiculous scenes which were enacted by those whose limbs we had, in times past, warmed by night and by day. This too which would make humanity blush if they were brought to light. But I have been wandering again. I will now confess, and come back to business. To return then to the subject of slave holder's religion, I will state that at a large and respectable Rag Convention, which was held at the paper mill, and of which I had the honor of being chairman, the Assembly in full convention came to the following conclusion, viz: That if my slave master, who was known as brother Cotton, was really the prime and sole owner of Aunt Dinah's soul, body, and spirit; he was also the owner of her offspring, in the same sense as he owned the old mare and her colt, and all there was in them or about them. If their exterior belonged to my master, the same bond would hold also their interior; the inner as well as the outer man. My brother Dirty Face then presented the following for the consideration of the assembly:

"Resolved, That if brother "Tell Tale Rag's" master had any right and lawful claim to Uncle Sam and Aunt Dinah, they were equally entitled to all the religion or grace said chattels might happen to possess in tneir hearts.

After which brother Shirt Sleeve presented the following resolutions as the sense of the meeting:

Resolved, That if human bondage be a heaven-ordained institution, that there is no class of people on earth who enjoy as much religion as southern slaveholders, as many of them hold at least from ten to one hundred of the true disciples of Michael, the prince of freedom.

Resolved, That if this platform should fail, and every man's work is to be tried by fire, that pro-slavery ministers, and all slave-holders would go to their own place, which in all probability would be an emigration to a more tropical clime than their chosen Carolinas.

This being the sense of the brethren assembled, it was unanimously adopted.

The assembly then broke up for the night, said their

prayers, and retired to rest after singing the following stanzas, in a peculiar metre, adapted to the hymn :

1 Hail happy rags of every hue,
In grave convention now assembled,
Hail to each glorious wig and cue,
That ever on slave driver trembled.

2 For thoughts profound, convened, we have
To prove, the Holder, and the slave,
To learn if each, or both be free
To claim true liberty and love.

3 To hold a slave, is right, or wrong,
The master's saved by *Chattel* graces,
Or slaves are safe upon the prong
Responsibility, the *Master's* place is.

4 If Pharaoh was a man of God,
And strawless tricks a just demand,
When on the Jews he laid the rod,
His rule was righteous in the land.

5 If Uncle Sam, and Dinah's child
Like the mare's colt, belonged to cotton,
It should be sung, the system mild,
In songs, and praises ne'er forgotten.

6 But if the slave a rightful claim
Has to himself, like Royal bloods,
Then shall the Lord, upon him rain,
Who would oppress them, fiery floods

7 Of wrath, and vengence from the clouds,
Which like a storming battery frowns,
And ever, Ah ! forever shrouds
The oppressors' right to golden crowns.

Perhaps it would be interesting to my reader, at this point, and while we have the subject of religion by the hand, to know the circumstance which aroused my master and mistress to the subject of religion, and to a preparation to meet their final account.

There was an old slave who had served my master faithfully in the cotton field until he was about four-score years old. He had walked, Enoch like, with God for half a century, through much tribulation, and "had this testimony, that he pleased God," and it always seemed a small matter to Uncle Harry, whether any one else was pleased with him or not. He now became too aged and infirm to labor, and so was left in his cabin, where he waited a few years for the "pale horse and his rider," who, with a single stroke would break the shell of his soul's prison-house, and wing his way to the land of the free, and the home of the brave. My master at this time was set down as one of the wealthiest men in his township. A merciful God, who has a thousand ways to arouse the slumbering energies of sinners, did in his case succeed in lifting the eyelids of his soul, by the following dream: In the visions of the night he saw a new dug grave; this happened previous to my birth, but I have often heard Uncle Sam speak of it while discussing his master's foundational hope of heaven. True, Uncle Sam considered it rather sandy, but I will relate the dream in its particulars:

Upon a time, about twelve o'clock at night, he dreamed that the richest man in the town of S. should die, precisely at nine o'clock the following day. He was startled, and awoke. It is true, said he, while soliloquizing a moment, that I am the richest man in town; he felt his pulse, found all right, and saying, this is nothing but a dream, reposed himself to sleep; at one o'clock he was again aroused by the repetition of his dream, when he said, oh fudge! I've no confidence in dreams, curled down again in the arms of Morpheus, and fell asleep.

At three o'clock precisely, he was effectually awakened by the same trackless, speechless messenger, who this time brought him to his feet. His flesh quivered on his bones, his teeth chattered, as he aroused the household and told them the terrible vision. His house was literally and spiritually, in disorder. How to make his will, and dispose of his earthly possessions, and how he should meet his account at the bar of a sin-avenging God, were thoughts which were crushed into a moment's time. Consequently, the lawyer was brought in haste to write his will, while close followed at his heels the probang minister, with his policy of insurance for his soul. My master then related to him that he had got all his property arrangements completed satisfactorily, "but, to tell the truth," said he, as he looked up in the face of the preacher, while his eyeballs rolled and his whole frame quivered, as if his heart was then the battle-field where the powers of freedom and slavery were crossing steel, "I have ever had compunctions of conscience and horrible doubtings concerning this slave-holding business, and was upon the point, like Freeborn Garretson, of breaking, with one stroke, every bond, and letting my slaves go free." It was one of the awfully critical moments of my life; the scales seemed hovering for five awful minutes on their fulcrum, but at that moment there seemed to be a whispering in my ear, "Will them all to your children; wash your hands, and if there should be any iniquity, the children must take the responsibility." "Amen!" shouted his spiritual adviser; "wisdom and righteousness have removed the guilt from your trembling hands. Give to the winds thy fears." By the time the probang could sprinkle some water on his fevered brow and sign him with the Cross, and so label him and salt him down, as a consignee would his cargo, for heaven, he, having thus joined the church, saw by the pointers on the old family clock that he had but three or four minutes more to stay. By this time the house was crowded with neighbors. His wife and children gathered close around him, and his physician kept his finger upon his pulse. "I'd assure you," said Uncle Sam, "it was an awful three minutes. My master's eye was transfixed upon the clock, and the mourning friends around the bed seemed afraid to breathe; and when the minute hand seemed to point directly to the upper and the nether world, the old hammer drew steadily back, and as it struck the bell, it was like the peal of the arch-angel startling the sheeted dead. It still continued until it struck nine. My master breathed, and breathed on. Just at that moment a messenger came running in and broke the awful silence by declaring that the moment the old clock struck nine, old black Harry fell from his chair and died, and thus it was decided who was the wealthiest man in the town of S———." And now, as I am nothing but a cast-off rag, and have no soul to save or lose, nor reputation to nurse, I can speak disinterestedly of the things which I have seen and heard.

My master and mistress were soon "confirmed," as Uncle Sam said, in their sins, went to church, bought a beautiful gilt-edged prayer-book, read prayers at church, and when it came to the place where the word "Amen" was printed, my master made the old church ring again with a hearty response. On Sabbath he partook of the Sacrament, and on Monday, if he was hard pushed for a thousand dollars, would sell that amount of "Hams" to the traders in flesh and blood. While that money lasted, my master's house was a continuous scene of banqueting and revelry for the blood families that would touch at his wharf, or surround his sumptuous table.

All this time, the probang minister and his dear family stood in clover to the chin; and, as Mrs. Stowe said, "on such occasions, when Aunt Chloe, the cook, entered the poultry yard, all the turkeys, ducks, &c., would look as solemn as the grave, knowing that their end was nigh;" and these "Hams" that were brought into market and sold in the slave shambles were, doubtless, some of them, members of the mystical body of our Lord Jesus Christ, so that in this view, my master seemed, from the time of this solemn warning, to grow worse, and to have taken in at least seven spirits, if possible worse than the first.

I can not think of closing this chapter without recurring to the patriarch Harry, as he lies upon the cabin floor. His fleecy locks were as white as the pure wool, in striking contrast with his deep-furrowed ebony face. I have heard Uncle Sam, while hoeing in the field, explain what the "Patriarch of Uz" meant when he compared aged Christians to a "shock of corn fully ripe in its season." You know, said he, that the corn which Massa intends for his own table use is left standing in the field all winter after it is fully ripe, as the more severe frostings it has, the sweeter will be the bread made from it. I have often looked at these fields of corn when the top stalk was cut off above the ear, and thought what a striking resemblance existed between the parted, faded husks and the fleecy heads of aged men and women. You may set a thousand of them by the side of a thousand hills of corn, not as yet gathered into the garner, and you will be forcibly struck with the fac simile before your eyes. Both have lost their greenness and verdure of youth, and while they have witnessed the husbandman gathering into their barns thousands of their neighbors, as soon as they come to their full stature, or the "full corn in the ear." This, to them, was very strange, why they themselves were left in the open fields to face so many wintry blasts, bear the beating of so many wintry winds, and be frozen and chilled by so many pinching frosts The secret, said Uncle Sam, lies here. They are reserved especially for bread for the master's table in heaven. They are not only ripe fruit, but dead ripe fruit. Dip a tumbler into the middle of the ocean and another into the broad bay at the mouth of the Hudson, and the saltness of the water in each will be nearly equal. This arises from the commingling occasioned by the ebbing and flowing of the sea. So it was with Uncle Harry. His soul had lived beneath the tides of God's love until he had partaken of his nature. The ebbing sea had carried him out into the deep, deep ocean of love; it was but a step. For years he had lingered in the vestibule of heaven. When his mouldy crust was thrown into his cabin in the morning, he could get down upon his knees, and, while tears of gratitude would overflow the furrows upon his dark face, he would exclaim,

"All this crust for unworthy Harry, and heaven besides." Then his guardian angel which attended him would whisper in his ear, "I know thy tribulation and thy poverty, but thou art rich;" while it might have also added, Thy master, in his lifetime, receiveth his good things, and thou thy evil things; now Harry is comforted, and he shall be tormented.

Many Christians, when they die, leave their poverty and go to their riches, while the ungodly leave all that they have, for "they have their portion in this life," and go to their extreme poverty and sorrow. Such, also, are some of the legalized fashionable sins in this secession domain where my first master resided.

CHAPTER FIFTH.

In this chapter we are to take our departure from the land of Egypt. This we will call our Exodus. Whatever our fate may be hereafter, we have no tears to shed, for our needle is already settled upon the northern star. But before we leave, I am desirous of explaining some more things which have puzzled many of the most pious of the latter-day saints. About this time, of which I am now writing, there was brought into the paper mill several sacks of rags which were gathered, as the others had been, from the four winds of heaven. Some of them had served as shirts, pants, coats, calicoes, night-gowns, night-caps, &c., &c. They were to us like fresh newspapers, powder-stained with the latest intelligence, telling us that war had already commenced in the United States. In them we learned that John Brown had made a foray, and buried several of the Egyptians in the sand at Harper's Ferry; that Moses had already taken his rod in his hand and commenced proclaiming the "Higher Law" in the courts of Pharaoh; that Michael had declared that his people should leave the brick yards, &c. So, take it all together, there was quite a time among the snakes and the rods. Jannes and Jambres, two of the secession generals, had seemed, at one time, to have defeated the embassador of Michael, who went forth under "sealed orders." But just at this time of the crisis, "I am, that I am" came to the relief of Moses, and, strange to tell, the serpentine rod of Moses opened its mouth widely, and swallowed at once every rod of these secessionists, spiked their cannon of strength, and consequently they were shorn of their power, thus showing, prophetically, how the kingdoms of this world shall all wheel into line at the command of Michael, the great prince, and the eternal principles of the "Higher Law" shall triumph as he bruises the head of the old usurper under his feet.

Let us now return to the paper mill, from which I

so frequently depart. Being so long accustomed to travel with my various masters, it is very hard to stay long in one place. All is alive and astir now, and we were, in one sense, like the disciples on the day of Pentecost, "All of one accord in one place." Another good feature was, there was with us no respecter of persons. The rag that had graced the symmetrical form of the city belle was just as humble as its neighbor, who had bandaged the gangrened shins of a drunkard. We had all been made perfect through suffering. That is, perfectly free from pride, codfish aristocracy, blue Phariseeism, &c., &c.

Being somewhat given to speech-making, it was agreed upon that another "Rag Convention" should be called, to which our new allies should be personally invited, as their additional intelligence would add greatly to the interest of the meeting. As I was the most aged member of the assembly, I was again honored as chairman, and the first question presented for the consideration of the body was, the reconciliation, if possible, of the clashing of the spiritual armor which is now heard in the household of faith. As to the clashing of carnal weapons between those who stood on the Abrahamic platform and the secessionists, there was no variety of opinions as to the cause; but when one member after another would rise in his place and tell how fervently his master would send up from his pulpit loud and long petitions unto the God of Abraham, Isaac and Jacob for the success of the Southern troops, and that their battle bow might abide in its strength, until every Northerner of abolition tendencies should be made to lick the dust of repentance and swear allegiance to the slave code; and *vice versa*, ministers and members of the same denominational name, praying for the success of the North; that God would draw the linch-pins from the chariot wheels of Pharaoh, and that confusion and dismay might enter every pigeon-hole of the brains of the secession leaders and counsellors, until the dove of peace should gently perch on every flag-staff of the Union, and all mankind be made free and equal. Another member, from the Border States, arose and gave the following illustration:

Suppose, said he, there was but one postoffice in heaven, and that eighteen millions of letters from the Northern States and twelve or thirteen millions from the Southern States should find their way daily into this general postoffice, and every one of them burthened with a petition to the King, praying for his divine aid, and committing their cause to him; and as the King could, with his all-seeing eye, read them all at once, and finding them perfectly antagonistic, clashing and crossing each other, a good share of them from his professed followers, what he would do with them was what puzzled the brains of the convention. As

God could not be divided nor have respect to persons, and is without partiality, but as he is exclusively partial to character and principles, without any reference to Mason and Dixon's, or any other geographical lines, was what most puzzled the convention, and left them to flounder in the troughs of this sea of conjecture.—At this point a little calico rag, which had been worn by a beautiful little girl, arose, and with some little timidity, asked leave of the Chair to address the convention. The little girl, said she, who was my daily companion, strayed with me one day, over the meadows and through ravines, in search of flowers. She gathered a large bunch of every kind she could find, intending them as a present to her mother. As she came back and showed them to her elder brother, who was working in the field, he took them in his hand and discovered that nearly one-half of them were blossoms from the most poisonous weeds that grew on the earth. These he drew out and cast them upon the ground, and the remainder he arranged into a beautiful boquet, which yielded the most grateful fragrance. Now, said he to his little sister, present that to our mother, and ten to one if you don't get showered with kisses and blessings. And this, said the calico rag, in my opinion, is the way Jesus does with all the prayers and petitions that come to his postoffice. Every one that does not come up in faith, perfumed in the merits of his blood, every one which does not accord with the principles of purity and freedom for soul and body, every one that does not plead for the oppressed and liberty to the captives, is thrown out and cast into the gulf of Gehenna, and the balance are placed in the golden censor and beautifully arranged, and then presented to the Father of Mercies by the Great High Priest, who is perpetually standing before the throne as our intercessor. Light now flashed upon the minds of every member of the assembly. Darkness was dissipated as by the rising sun, and the convention closed by singing the following heart-cheerers:

"Brethren, don't you hear the sound,
  Abram's trumpet now is blowing;
Men in orders listening round,
  And soldiers to the standard flowing.

Oh, ye Rebels, now desist,
  The officers are now recruiting;
Why will you in sin persist,
  Or waste your time in vain disputing.

All excuses now are vain;
  For if you do not sue for favor,
Down you'll sink to endless pain,
  And bear the wrath of God forever.

Hark! the victors shouting loud,
  Freedom's chariot-wheels are rumbling,
Slavers weeping through the crowd,
  Secession's kingdom down is tumbling.

Dear Reader: We have wept with those who weep thus far on our journey, as we have looked upon some of the outlines of the slave system; but you must not pocket your handkerchief yet, for we have another picture to present before you, which should break up every fountain of your sympathetic nature. We are now to introduce to you, before we quit the cotton-field, my slave-holding master's own children, with the rose and lily beautifully blended upon their cheeks. They are, if possible, to be pitied more than the sons and daughters of Ham. 'Tis true that their backs have not been plowed in deep furrows by the slave-driver's lash, but they have been fed with the poison of asps from their infancy. Doctrines and principles, demoralizing in the extreme, have been taught them, and they start in the race of life with a lie in their right hand. As soon as they know their right hand from their left, they are addressed by the gray-headed slave and the stripling as "Young Massa" and "Young Missus," and this distinction of master and slave takes deep root in the youthful bias of their hearts, and grows with their growth, until it becomes a poisonous Upas, spreading its deadly branches as far as their influence may extend. Beneath this tree lie bleached bones, for it is the charnel house of licentious tyranny and vain glory. Nothing can flourish beneath its branches that will bless the world or colonize the bright fields of glory.

You can easily convince these children that the baker

can, from the same flour barrel, mould the plain loaf of bread, from the same dough make a pie, a baby cake, a dog, a horse, and forty other things; but when you tell them that the great Creator has made all flesh from the same material — that the slaveholder and the slave, horses, hogs and dogs, are all made from the same flour barrel, or, in other words, that dust is the common material from which all are made — this is too humiliating to believe; they are puffed up with the idea that the all-wise Creator has moulded them from the fine flour in the head of the bolt, the common white peasantry from the middlings, the negroes from the bran. Henceforth, from this cursed leaven, hid in the meal of aristocracy and royal blood, springs forth the results which follow to those who, sowing to the flesh, are doomed to reap the terrible reward of an endless corruption. Nothing which man can do upon the earth will bring down the wrath of a sin-avenging God upon them, can equal the crime of being a respecter of persons, or despising the work of the Creator's hands. There is no sin, North or South, in the church or out of the church, more common, more fashionable, more damning at the present day; one, too, of which my first master and mistress were terribly guilty.

Uncle Sam has often illustrated high life and low life by quoting the apostle, who says that "in every

"Oh, massa," says Uncle Sam, "I splain all dat ar. S'pose rich man make a feas', an' say everybody come an' eat. Massa an' I come to de door. togedder, an' massa, he great learnin', stan' at de door, an' stan', an' splain all 'bout de blosofy, how de turkey an' de onions grow, an' talk all 'bout de odder good tings. Ole Sam, he no learnin'; he go straight in, take up de carvin' knife, cut off de turkey's leg, dig out de stuffin', pour out de gravy, den reach roun', pile on de good tings, open his mouf wide, as de Bible says; bye and bye he git full up to de neck; den 'gin to crack de nuts, drink de wine, git downright happy, an' shout an' bress de Lord. An' all massa do, stan' out an' splain. Dat's de way ole Sam does at de spiritual feas' dat massa Jesus make in de ole cabin.

CHAPTER SIXTH.

My master about this time had set up a whiskey distillery, which caused the opening of several slime pits of sodom in the neighborhood. He saw that the ship was sinking, and so went into merchandising also.—He got trusted with goods to the amount of fifty thousand dollars; kept two or three race horses for the turf, opened a cock pit, and a gambling saloon. With these carcasses, the Turkey Buzzards, and every other foul biped assembled; banqueting, revelry, and debauching in high life, were the orders of the day, until the ship was about scuttled ; a mortgage on the whole plantation for about its value gave temporary relief.—At length the New York merchants' bill of fifty thousand dollars became due, and no money was to be had to meet the claim, consequently a chattel mortgage was given as collateral security, on all the personal chattels, such as horses, cows, hogs, negroes, cotton crop, &c.; all this while these mortgages were kept secret from the public, as also from my master's own family; so he was still considered the wealthiest man in the town.—But in the midst of all this revelry in high life among the parlor furniture, they little dreamed what a day would bring forth. Thus matters went on, until one day after a season of unusual debauch, the die was to be cast, and the plot developed. At midnight, following this ominous day, the silence of the plantation was broken by the announcement that my master had fallen, while in a state of intoxication, from one of his race horses, and broken his neck. It was something like the night when the destroying angel smote the first born in Egypt, for its terrors. From the mud hovel in the rear of the mill, to the palace of the royal bloods, there came forth a spontaneous howl throughout the land. It was customary among the Egyptians to have their mourning and howling done by proxy. 'Tis most likely that the widow and her children would gladly have availed themselves of this substitution, had it been the fashion of the country; but as hard work as it was to mourn, and bring out tears, they did rend several yards of crape, and hang it upon their persons, and tie several white napkins on the arms of their slaves. This made quite an impression at the funeral. I would not have you think that the children were without natural affection, but they were comforted in this sad hour by a tingling on the ends of their fingers, in the prospect of the immediate seizure of, at least a cool hundred thousand dollars of the inheritance.

The fair daughters, especially, who were then in market, could console their lovers, or fan to a perfect blaze their conjugal fires, by saying, "Our Father who art in Heaven." So there would be no long and tedious waiting for the old man to give up the ghost, and the inheritance, by saying, "thy will be done," "give us the portion that falleth to us of the inheritance." I observed that not a little jealousy had been already awakened among the children, even before the last kind offices had been performed by the sexton in arranging the green turf upon the grave.

The question was, how the slaves should be divided among them.

At this awful juncture, I must for a few minutes clip my thread, to tell you of a contract between my master and Uncle Sam as he entered the cotton field one day. He being filled with the spirit—I mean the spirit that courses its way through the undying copper worm in the old distillery—for on such occasions he would often be very religious, so much so as to condescend to talk to men of low estate, and think, and talk something about dying, and often mingle humanity's tears with the sons of Ham, losing sight of his royal blood, and pedigree: "Sam," said he, "if I die first, you must preach my funeral sermon, and from that hour you and Dinah shall have your freedom;" and I would remark, in proof of his sincerity, that Uncle Sam and Dinah were reserved in the stipulations of the mortgage. But to resume: Master was now dead, and this was the hour of trial for Uncle Sam. It was the Cross and Freedom alternately revolving in his mind. Although, when working with his own harness on, with an audience of kitchen furniture, in cabin or at Camp Meeting, he was a "son of thunder," in prayer he would bring heaven and earth together, and cause the pillars of darkness to tremble, and the saints to cry aloud for joy, his skeleton, in preaching, if he had any, was so fat that his audience could neither see nor feel the ribs.

But this preaching to parlor furniture, who generally criticise instead of pray, was a new business altogether to Uncle Sam

But the thought of his freedom was, to him, next to his hope of heaven, and overcoming all scruples he mounted the platform which was erected for the occasion. He was full six feet tall in his stockings, and well proportioned; the model of a mighty man. His white fleece and sable skin were set off in beautiful contrast; but the sermon and the preacher must be heard and seen to be understood and appreciated. I shall not attempt, dear reader, more than an outline of the sermon. He first related the contract between himself and his master, as an apology for the position which he then occupied. The text I have forgotten, but he proceeded to say something as follows:

"De fust ting dat I shall 'tempt to say is dat everybody's got to die. If you don't b'lieve dis, jus look dar in dat coffin, whar ole massa lies wid his neck broke. De next ting is to show up some ob de good quality ob my massa. Ebrybody," said he, "know dat my massa keep de best game-cock, an' de best race-hoss, an' make de best whisky in ole Carolina. An' O Lor! help ole Sam to tell de odder part ob de story. Ebrybody knows, too, dat my ole massa would drink whisky, cock-fight, an' run de hosses on de Lor's day. An' lastly, whar is ole massa gwine to? Dat I may comfort de mourners is de hardest ting eber one poor nigger had to do."

At this juncture of the case, the cold sweat stood in

large drops on his ebony face, and he paused for a moment, as he dropped his hook deep down into the sea, hoping that some fish would come up with an idea in its mouth which would save him from breaking down, losing his reputation as a preacher, hazarding his freedom, and sending the mourners away without a drop of comfort or a rag of hope that the deceased had gone to the better land. But the fish came at last, with the best consolation that could be found.

"Ah," said Uncle Sam, "dar is one passage ob Scripture dat say dat dar be many mansions in Hebben, an' who knows but dat dar is one mansion for de distiller, anoder for de hoss-racer, anoder for de cock-fighter an' gamblers. If dat is so, den my ole massa has a share in all ob dem, an' all ob you as want to see ole massa, jus walk de same way an' you will find him dar. An' dis is de best ole Sam can do for you poor mourners an' all dese good gentle folks."

I have thought that if all funeral sermons could be preached as honestly as this was, there would be fewer sinners in the world. If an inhabitant of some other planet should visit our earth, and hear nothing but the funeral sermons, read the newspaper obituaries and the poetry on the tomb-stones, he would surely report that every body died Christians on this earth and went straight to glory. This is another fashionable, popular and cursed sin of the day.

But we must prepare for leaving, for I perceive that the mortgage is foreclosed on the plantation, and blazing handbills are stuck upon every post, announcing an auction sale of all the horses, cattle, negroes and cotton, in virtue of the mortgage of the New York merchant. The glorious expectations of the heirs were blasted, and they were like a peacock when looking at its feet, whose plumage drops at once. Poor things! they and their banqueting friends had swallowed down their necks the whole plantation, with a hundred negroes, and other chattels. They were by this time neither fit for parlor nor kitchen furniture. All their blazing fires of connubial affection from moustached swains were quenched at once. Dig, they could not; to beg they were ashamed. Let him who hath tears to shed, drop them along the pathway of a planter's children who are reared, or rather *grow* up, on slave soil, a lot of spoiled eggs. But I see the traders in blood are gathering in, the slave coffles are filling up, hearts of mothers and children begin to bleed, and, strange to say, our old probang minister has laid down his religious probang for the auctioneer's hammer.— His tongue runs as glibly as a mill-clapper, and he cries out, "What will you give?" Here a scene follows that beggars description, as parental cords are severed and the slaves are hitched to the various gang-chains to be taken where, they know not. As for myself, I was crowded, with my white-headed companions, into a sack and bid in by the New York merchant, and, for the first time, we realized the goodness of our Creator in forming us without nerves, otherwise we could not have witnessed the awful scenes of the day without weeping our lives away, or squirming out of the sack. But here we go into the railroad cars and bid farewell to Southern Egypt.

Our next address will be in the great store-house of my new master, under the cognomen of Cotton Professor, who resides in New York a part of the season, and travels extensively through the entire Southern States, or, at least, has done so.

MY SECOND MASTER.

CHAPTER SEVENTH.

Gentle reader, before we introduce our second master, into whose hands we have now fallen, permit me to give a little sketch of our journey on the way to our American London. My companions with myself were as joyful and happy chums as were ever chucked together in a sack, notwithstanding we were leaving the land that gave us birth. Our joy was not unlike that of the two hundred thousand virgins who were dancing a quadrille on the green, amid the striking of timbrels and shouts of triumph that arose from a million lookers-on, as they celebrated the day of their deliverance from bondage, and the departure down below of their enemy. We all look back upon the glories of the old plantation, which, like ancient Egypt, was blasted and blighted. To finish up the judgment of a righteous God, the locusts and caterpillars devoured every green thing, and the Israelites left while Egypt wailed for her first born. It was under similar circumstances that we left our slave-land. Pompous pride, laziness and good-for-nothingness, connected with every species of extravagance, both of the toilet and table, in my master's family, brought them to ruin. Add to this the swarms of visitors, who were about as plentiful as the locusts and caterpillars of Egypt, and had swallowed up every green thing that had life, including all the living "Hams" of the plantation; and when it was too late, they prayed, "O Lord, deliver us from our friends." From a spiritual point of view there was another striking similarity to the ancient slave-land, in the midst of the blackness of darkness and the wailings for their first born. There was the little city of Goshen, the inhabitants of which lived in humble mud houses. On the lintels of each of the doors was a blood-red sprinkle; it was the king's seal, as much as to say, no pestilence or death shall come near thy dwelling. Strange to tell, while the marble fronts and palaces of the slave-holding nobility were filled with darkness and death, every mud house in Goshen, like the body of a true believer, was filled with brilliant light, and every one of the inmates was sound and healthy, not a sick or feeble one among them.—They seemed to be "minute men," with their loins girded about and their staves in their hands, waiting for marching orders. Moreover, they were feasting upon a roasted lamb, together with bitter herbs, as much as to say, if any of you feast by faith on the Lamb of God, you shall reign with him. The bitter herbs, Uncle Sam used to say, are emblemtical of our suffering with him. This is the principal reason why infidels will not come to the feast; they do not like the bitter herbs that grow and twine around the cross.—We farther find, in looking in the old family record, that these Goshenites were the children of Abraham, and that Michael had made a contract with the patriarch that, with his aid, he should colonize the land of Canaan.

While we have had many hard things to say about our neighbors in our Southern Egypt, we are still happy to inform our readers that there is a Goshen even in that benighted country, and that in the log cabins and some of the castles, Michael, the great prince, has been, and is this day, amid the clashing of arms and garments died in blood, colonizing the plains of glory with a host no man can number. What were counted kitchen, or dishonorable furniture, down in the old grave yard, are now counted as of more value, and are seated in the ante-chamber of the king, and in the golden parlors of heaven. "Though thy dwelling," saith the prophet, "hath been among the pots and kettles, yet will I make thee as the dove whose wings are silver and whose feathers are pure gold."

But here we are, a hundred miles from our starting place already. The ride has been novel in the extreme to us all, as we were but "green-horns from the country." Some of us thought, as we passed by the marble mile-stones so frequently, that we must be going through an everlasting grave yard full of tombstones. Some called our iron horse "a cold water teetotaler," as cold water was his exclusive drink; and others named him the "old Southern fire-eater," as fire seemed to be his sole diet, which he devoured freely without giving him the dyspepsia; and had not his maker, who gave him such a fearful and wonderful form, made him, in mercy, like ourselves, without any nerves, we might drop a sympathizing tear in consequence of the unmerciful manner in which the postillion lashed him over the track. But as it was getting late, we all concluded to say our prayers, that Uncle Sam and Aunt Dinah taught us in the cotton-field, and sing the following hymn we learned from the children of Ham, and woke up just as we touched the citv wharves:

TUNE—*Auld Lang Syne.*

"What are the joys of the white man here?
What are his pleasures, say?
He great, he proud, he haughty, fine,
While I my banjo play.
He sleep all day, he wake all night,
He full of care, his heart no light,
He great deal want, he little get,
He sorry, so he fret.

Me envy not the white man here,
  Though he so proud and gay;
He great, he proud, he haughty, fine,
  While I my banjo play.
    Me work all day, me sleep all night,
    Me have no care, me heart is light,
    Me think not what to-morrow bring,
    Me happy, so me sing."

Good gracious, exclaimed the crew, as we were roused from our slumbers by a dozen steamboat bells; while a hundred paddle wheels stirred Old Neptune to the agitation of a boiling chaldron; together with a thousand omnibusses thundering over the pavements; as old mother Royal would say, our voyage was "like a transition from Hell to Heaven."

The king of day had by this time wrapped his bridal robes around him, and coming forth from his eastern chamber tinged with gold, the stately domes that pierced the blue sky of the morning, to welcome us amidst the homes of the free.

We were now carted along the main streets to our destined lodgings. If the living mass of beings which we met, had been quadrupeds, we should have supposed we were meeting Jacob, with his drove returning to the old homestead, in Hebron. They were ring-streaked and speckled, grizzly grey, and brown; all nations, kindreds and tongues.

But it is high time we had an audience with our new master. Well, here he comes, with his gold mounted cane, gold spectacles, with their bows piercing his silver grey locks. He is, reader, what some of our abolition editors have styled, sarcastically of course, a "Cotton Professor." A name, in my opinion more odious than "Tell Tale Rag." It is true, my new master holds the highest seat in the synagogue, and is always found in the uppermost rooms at feasts. But as I am pledged to drag into day light the secret sins of my first masters, loud and long though be their prayers; *he is a wicked slave holder*, and the sacred pages of the old family bible that lies on the stand, are besmeared with the prints of his bloody hands; yes, while he is standing and praying, and lifting up unholy hands, with both wrath and doubting, he is commanding his lips and tongue to ask God to deliver the captives—to break every yoke of the oppressor—yes, while he is doing this both his hands are stretched across Mason and Dixon's line, and clenched into the wool of whole plantations of slaves; by virtue of his chattel mortgages, he will drag them to the block of the auctioneer, and from thence to the trader's gang chain.

From this scene he will return to the city with his filthy lucre, on every dollar of which should be stamped an "Aceldama," and instead of buying a "Potter's field" a portion of it will buy him the highest seat in the synagogue; Uncle Sam used to say, that these northern-light slave holding professors of every denomination will receive the greater damnation. It is very difficult for the church and for the world to know what to do with such professors of religion, unless they let them hang suspended by attraction like Mahomed's coffin, between Heaven and Hell, not exactly fitted for either place. To illustrate their position let me relate a circumstance which happened in my first master's family.

They were at one time preparing to entertain an unusually large company, and fearing they had not a sufficient number of trained house servants to meet the demand of table waiters, they brought in some raw "Hams" from the field the day previous to the assembly for my mistress to train, by practicing with empty plates. Among the raw "Hams" was old Betty, she could handle the hoe to perfection, she knew how to roast an Opossum, and sop the "Hoe Cake" in the fat; but to wait on quality at the table of a southern blood, was as much out of her line as was Uncle Sam's pulpit at the funeral of his master.

My mistress's first instructions were, to be sure and hand all her plates on the right hand of the guests; and fearing she might forget which the right hand side was, she instructed Betty to pass the plate on the side that had buttons on, the gentlemen's coats, as it was then the fashion to wear single breasted coats, had but a single row of buttons, and those were on the right side.

The hour came when the extensive and luxurious banquet was to be spread; the first dish to be served, in order, was a deep plate of vanilla soup. Old Betty performed or served several plates to perfection, until she came to a northern yankee who had buttons on both sides, having on a double breasted coat; old Betty was now thrown into the utmost confusion as she passed the plate alternately from one side to another, alternately sprinkling the guest with the soup; till finally in her distress she cried out "good Lordy, missus, what shall I do now? here is a gemman got buttons on both sides he coat." There are also thousands of politicians and professors who have buttons on both sides of their coat, and it is impossible to know which side to hand the soup.

They are also like the luke-warm Laodaceans, neither cold nor hot; they are like Epicac, or tepid water in the stomach, and until they are spewed out of the church, the daughter of Zion will be sickly and consumptive. I had rather see a man like the good old deacon, when he prayed.

It seems that there were two brothers who at their father's death became joint heirs to "Old Pomp," the only slave their father had to will them; now as Pomp could not be divided without some inconvenience to himself; the two brothers agreed that Pomp should serve them alternately every other week. Now the deacon being a good man, had his family altar, as the head of every family should have, and as he bowed down between "Pomp" and his mistress, after telling the Lord what a great king he was, then came along and prayed for the restoration of the Jews, which brought him nearly to the close of the first half hour in prayer, after which he would wind up in a most pathetic manner, asking the Lord to bless him and his dear wife, and his half of "Pomp."

Now I do believe, that such men are safer to trust with, either the true riches or the unrighteous mammon than these "weather cock professors," or "majority politicians." When the devil dwelling in Balak failed through Balaam to get an enchantment against Jacob, from time to time, he at last succeeded in blowing to a flame the conjugal proclivities of the sons and daughters of the Israelites and Canaanites; knowing that God had strictly forbidden their intermarriage, or any intercourse whatsoever; nevertheless he continued to throw on the splinters, so congenial to the flesh, until the connubial fires from youthful hearts blazed like a brush heap, and flame mingled with flame, until the interests of the two nations were completely interwoven in one web of matrimony. They thus trampled under their feet one of Jehovah's commands, until a breach being made through their walls, the devil rushed in with his aliens and thus brought Jacob into captivity. Precisely in the same manner has the devil sought to destroy the Methodist church, as also other denominations. The free-women's children of the north have been married to the bond-women's children of the south, and thus their children have become half-breeds. If John Wesley or Ancient Ham should seek for their children, they would find too many of them, looking too much like Dr. Hooker, or Ham's posterity, with the kinks of their hair nearly straightened out; and his Hams very poorly smoked, or faded nearly white.

"Know ye not that he who is joined to a Harlot is the same flesh?" and worst of all, their nuptial festivities have been grand, and sanctioned by the High Priests, and the Levites that serve at the altar. They have also baptized their children and mingled their names with those who are born of the incorruptible seed; checked their baggage or sins which they carry along with them, and ticketed them for the pearly gates of the city. Uncle Sam said, that they would meet with the same reception at this gate as John Bunyan's pilgrims did that started from the land of "Vain Glory," and tumbled over the wall into the king's highway. But we must close this already too long chapter.

"He that is down need fear no fall,
He that is low, no pride,
He that is humble ever shall
Have God to be his guide."

CHAPTER EIGHTH.

I see by the morning papers that we are all to be sold to-morrow at auction, so I must take a "French leave" of my new master and look for another. But before we take the parting hand, I feel it to be my duty to explain a little farther the reasons why the church to which my Uncle Sam belonged should be stigmatized with the cotton odium, or why my present master should be introduced to you as a cotton professor. In explanation, then, I remark that it was in consequence of the mixed material of which his clothing is composed. The God and Father of the true Israel has always been very particular that his children should have a uniformity in dress, and has strictly forbidden them to adorn themselves with many things customary among the children of the wicked one.—Among other things, they were forbidden to wear garments composed of a thread of linen and a thread of woolen, or in modern times, a thread of cotton and a thread of woolen, as the fire is to try all our Christian virtues, or outward professions. To illustrate: I was reading in the papers the other day, or rather heard read, the following awful catastrophe;

Two men were sleeping together in the third story of a wooden building. One of them was clad in an all-wool shirt and drawers; his bed-fellow's shirt and drawers were composed of a thread of wool and a thread of cotton. At midnight a cry was made that the building in which they were lodging was wrapped in flames. They both leaped from the bed and undertook to dash through the flames to the door. The one with the all-wool garments escaped with little or no damage, while his bed-fellow, clad in his mixture, was devoured in the flames. The fire, seizing the cotton threads, ran like lightning over and through the garments, and the poor man fell down in the flames and perished.

We see this every day among the spiritual adulterers and adulteresses in the church, whose friendship is for the world, who undertake to mix up religion with the world, to intermarry freedom and slavery, Christ and Belial, light with darkness; when the old rugged cross is presented they are offended, scorched to death; not wool enough to save them from the flames. Ministers, too, that undertake to work in wood, hay and stubble among the lively precious stones in order to increase the numbers of their spiritual adherents, will also find that they have suffered a loss, when the fires shall try every man's work, of what sort it is. Some of the churches, for the last fifteen years, have been endeavoring to separate, or draw out the threads of cotton from the threads of wool; likewise, northern politicians have "sued for a divorce," and this is the principal cause of the crossing of the deadly weapons on the battle-field and in the church. The bondwoman's children can never live in peace with the free woman's children. They will quarrel, whether they are on the earth or under the earth. They would quarrel were it possible for them to be together in heaven or hell. This attempt at spiritual amalgamation is another fashionable sin of the day.

But I see that the red flag is hung out, and the buyers and sellers are crowding around us; they are the princes of this world. At their backs great wheels are set in motion, and a hundred thousand spindles pull our hair and twist our locks into a thousand kinks, like Uncle Sam's fleece. These men, too, are married into the same family of my present master, so you see we are not yet cleared from those who deal in the souls of men. The audience were mostly silver-gray-headed, heavily freighted with the cares of this world, and ready to cry out, with the rich man spoken of in the Gospel, "What shall I do? my store-houses and barns will not contain my abundant wealth." An auction was not a new thing to us, nor were buyers and sellers a strange auditory; but we were all startled by the well known voice of our probang preacher, who, being turned out of his stewardship, had made friends of the mammon of unrighteousness, and had changed the Gospel trumpet for the auctioneer's hammer, giving it a heavy rap upon the counter, as much as to say, All things are now ready.

At this moment, a tall, gimlet-eyed Yankee made his way to our side. The inordinate love of wealth had absorbed all the milk of human kindness he had about him, and he was as dry as a pelican in the wilderness. So without waiting for an introduction to us, gray-headed though we were, he drew forth from his pocket a dirk-knife, and gave us a kind of fifth rib stab. It was like the rent in Cæsar's mantle. He then thrust in his long fingers and jerked out some of our white locks, saying to himself, "First quality; equal to the stock from which John Brown's halter was made." The terrible hammer then fell, and we knew that he was to be our next master. We were soon mounted on a wheel-barrow in great haste, as the Eastern steamer, by her heavy breathing, declared that she should soon leave the wharf for the Pemberton Mills, the home and property of my new master.—Now, reader, you will suffer me to relate a little disaster that befell me and my brethren on the outset of our journey. 'Tis an old saying, "There is many a slip 'twixt the cup and the lip." But our slip was between the wharf and the steamer. A poor man who was wheeling us had borrowed a barrow, hoping to earn a shilling to buy bread for his dependent family. By some means the gang-plank slipped and precipitated porter, wheel-barrow and contents into the water. We, being light and buoyant, floated like a duck on the agitated surface, while the wheel-barrow and porter sank to the bottom like stones, as neither understood the art of swimming. The alarm cry from hundreds of voices, from boat and wharf, that a man was drowning, set every nerve a-fluttering like a jewsharp. No one knew who he was; he was no one's father, nor husband; nothing but a porter. He arose on the surface of the water once or twice, and none would dive after him. At last a man was seen to pitch into the water. All eyes were strained, expecting him to come up with a drowned man; but, to their astonishment, the man arose with his wheel-barrow which he had lent to the porter. Hope had given place to despair; all thought the man must be lost. Just at this moment a young sailor, hearing, at a distance, that a man was drowning, leaped into the crowd, cast off his "jerkin of blue," doffed his tarpaulin, and pitched into the sea. Directly he came up with his treasure, the porter, who, after some rolling and rubbing, recovered his consciousness and exclaimed, "Where is the man who saved my life? I want to see him, and give him my hand and all I have." The sailor gave him his hand, telling him that he was a thousand times paid, and then conveyed himself away. When my new master heard the cry, "a man drowning," he felt no alarm, but when he found his loved cotton-heads in jeopardy, the life-boat was let down and money freely offered for our rescue. Soon we found ourselves securely stowed in the hold of the ship, and paddling for Pemberton Mills. Now, when the ship's company had fallen asleep in the arms of Morpheus and my companions of the cotton-field to the land of Nod, I gave myself to reflection. It was a night, solitary, but clear, and adapted for thinking. The circumstance of a man, a wheel-barrow and a cotton bale being dropped into the water and being rescued, was, it is true, a common, every-day occurrence, and scarcely worth relating, unless we are, by its occurrence, enabled to drop our hook down deep into the sea, and hook up some principle or idea which our gentle reader can crowd into the pigeon-hole or archives of his or her brain that may be useful and profitable to them in after life. Peter, you know, at the command of Jesus, upon a time when neither of them had money enough to pay their taxes, dropped his hook into the sea and brought up a bull-head, which had in its mouth a sufficiency for this purpose.

But as I have now a nibble at my hook, I will draw in my line and see what we have got. It is a single word, a monosyllable; yet capacious enough to contain the sun, moon and stars, and fill heaven and earth. 'Tis LOVE! love to God and man. 'Tis the golden link that connects the emigrant train to the locomotive which goes to colonize the fields of glory. On this single word hangs all the law and the prophets. But this question has arisen in my mind, Which of the three loved the most, the sailor that delivered the strangling stranger, the man who took his life in his hand and dove after the wheel-barrow, or the love which swelled the heart of my master at the rescue of his loved ones in the cotton sack? They all seemed filled with inexpressible joy at our several deliverances, almost equal to that in the banqueting hall when the prodigal son had returned. I therefore came to this conclusion, that love was love, and its principles and operations always the same; and the measure and amount of all love may always be estimated in exact proportion to the sacrifice made to gain the object of that love. The extreme boundary of a man's self-love may be ascertained if you can get the measure of his under-jacket, or waistband to his small-clothes; that of a lady's self-love by the inner boundaries of her corsets. Charity is never suffered to overleap the boundaries of selfishness.

The sailor's love was akin to divine love; it knew no bounds; his bosom swelled like that of the author of all true love, seeking not his own welfare but the comfort and salvation of another. If the man who dived for the wheel-barrow, had perchance caught hold of the drowning man, instead of his wheel-barrow, while he scrambled at the bottom of the sea; he would have relaxed his grasp at once, and mentally exclaimed, for he could not speak in the water: "thou art not the object of my love," and would have felt about again for his wheel-barrow, and have brought it up with as much joy as if it were a child from his own fireside.

It was so with my master. If the whole ship's crew had gone down, while myself and companions were saved he would never have shed a tear, and we might have sung:

"The arms of love that encompass us,
Would all the cotton world embrace."

I have thought while lifting the veil of the future, that if these self-lovers could by any means climb over the walls of the city, and get into heaven, that they would be strangers even there; that if they wore a crown at all, it would be a starless one. The first man that the drowned porter enquired for, when resuscitated was the friend whose love went out of himself and caused him to dive into the sea, and restore him to his happy wife and children.

She was ready to smother him almost with kisses of gratitude, and to shower him with blessings, for his unfeigned love in restoring a dear father and husband.

How many will want to hunt up St. Paul, Luther,

Calvin, Wesley, Judson, and a host of others, as they open their eyes in glory, who had searched after them in the sea of depravity and tears; and who through grace have been brought to the shores of immortality.

While these lovers of gold, as some one has said, would dig up the pavements of the celestial city; for whatever they loved here the most they would love there most. The transition or change of a person's place of abode, does not change his loves or disposition.

Love is a passion, implanted in the human breast, which once was wholly right and holy in its aspirations, but it has now grown up into the degenerate plant of a strange vine. Ere sin entered into the world love was wholly centered in God. Then the fire burned purely, and the soul ascended in the sacred flame to the beatitudes of heaven. Then there was intercourse between heaven and earth, and man maintained a sweet communion with his maker. While admiring the beauties of creation, his soul could with pleasure ascend the streams of created excellencies, to the fountain of uncreated light and glory.

Ravished with the view, he saw his interest in his maker to be of another kind than this lower world could furnish. His experience was bliss, it was this experience which made Paradise the type of, and the vestibule of heaven itself.

It was this, and not the blooming flowers; this, and

not the verdant groves; this, and not the spreading stream; this, and not the fragrant gums; this, and not the bough bending with their spontaneous and perpetual fruits; this, and not the warbling birds, the chanting praises; this, and not the cloudless sky; this, and not the sight of angels; this, and not merely the mutual loves of our first parents; this it was which made Paradise what it was, and Adam and Eve, acceptable to God. But as we are drawing nigh our destined post, I must, on account of the consequent confusion close this chapter.

MY THIRD MASTER.

CHAPTER NINTH.

Well, here we are, touching the wharf of the Merrimac, the residence of my new master at the celebrated Pemberton Mills. Now the drayman is rattling us over the pavements to where I and my companions are to suffer all manner of persecutions, and then, perhaps, be separated from each other, and scattered like the leaves of autumn. Our next meeting may be in the scavenger's rag bag, or at the general assembly at the paper mill. After all, this may turn out for the best; for when the early christians were torn from each other and scattered to the four quarters of the globe, both men and women, they went out preaching from house to house and from city to city, so that the few ears of corn which were sent out from Lebanon have cast their seed over a good share of the earth, and are fast filling the garners of the better land.

This was a great mistake on the part of the old secessionist, for I and my brethren are sent out to warm ten thousand limbs, and, when we are cast off as rags, our indignant tongues will expose their secrets, and make some of them blush for their abuse of us. The factory bells are now hastily tapping, as much as to say, "leave off your unfinished meals, ye drudging spinsters, and pay your obeisance again to your jennies and looms." At once the streets of Pemberton, as if there had been a resurrection, were crowded with blooming maidens, up to their knees in bloomers. Thinks I to myself, this would be a smart chance for some of our southern boys to get an industrious wife; a wife, too, that would carry out the design of our Creator, to be a "help-meet," instead of a help-eat-meat. They would not send their husbands to bed, after a "Gaily the Troubadour" on the piano, for supper; nor he, like one of those southern plants which looks as pale as a potato stalk grown in the cellar, and who thinks it so cruel that the flies and musquitos, that continually annoy them, have no more respect for them than they have for the children of Ham.

After all, if a young man should come to select a wife among so many, he would be sorely puzzled in making a choice. For there he would be, his mind divided and sub-divided, and Cupid shooting arrows at him from a hundred points at once. It might turn out with him as it did with a little boy of my acquaintance. The first penny which he ever owned, he took to a toy shop to invest in some rare thing which he expected there to find. He went, and saw so many things that he wanted, that it puzzled him to know or tell which he wanted most; and so he left the shop with the penny in his hand, as rich as when he went. I suppose you have read in the Bible where there was a wholesale, or rather grab-game courtship in Shiloh. There were four hundred maidens leaping a quadrille on the green, and not a man or a married lady was amongst them. It was purely a religious worship, as practiced by the heathen. At this period in the history of Israel the sword of judgment had drank the last drop of female blood in the tribe of Benjamin, and in the excitement of the terrible conflict the other tribes had sworn, "Cursed is he that giveth his daughter to Benjamin." Therefore, to perpetuate the tribe, the following expedient was resorted to: Four hundred young Benjamites, anticipating the hour of the dance, secreted themselves in ambush, and, in the midst of the jumping and leaping of the quadrille, the leader of the Benjamites gave a signal, sprung the net, and very soon each lad had seized a lassie, swung her gently upon his back, or supported her upon his hip with his right arm tenderly compassing her waist, and thus they all were soon seated side by side in the tents of

Benjamin, where the nuptial rites were celebrated.—The Scripture does not give any account of any screaming, or fainting, or hysterics; no long and tedious courtship. This peculiar marriage was no doubt planned in heaven and consummated on the earth, and so the tribe of Benjamin was preserved.

True love matches make more than willing captives, and while I contemplated this Scripture narrative, I thought what an interesting picture it would be to see three thousand of these blooming maidens, so fearfully and beautifully made, carried off in like manner.—When young men go a fishing for a wife, they generally put themselves on the hook for a bait, and are doomed to wait until they can get a nibble or a bite; and there are some fish that can be only caught in a net, or captured with a spear.

Dear me, how long we have tarried in the streets of Pemberton, looking at these pretty girls and expatiating upon the untiring theme of courtship and marriage. After all, it is a heavenly theme, and we shall not make any apologies to any dry pelicans of bachelors.

But here we go, heels over head, into the storehouse. Now, the secret and besetting sins of my present master are three of the popular and fashionable sins of the present time. He was a Fusionist in politics, a Compromiser, in religion, with the old secessionist, and a seductive trapper in trade, transforming cotton into woolen. These were the three cardinal principles which permeated the whole man. They were like the three confederate kings of Sodom, who took Lot and his family captive, and would have enslaved them forever, had not Abraham at that time filled the Presidential chair. But, notwithstanding his deep piety and familiar friendship with Michael, his religion did not take all the fight out of him; but he at once summoned his invincible Zouaves, lashed on their swords, and soon spoiled the spoilers of their slaves, and brought them back to their God-given freedom, while these slaveholders found a very smooth and slippery gate to perdition through the slime-pits of Sodom.

Although I am a cast-off rag, and regarded as worthless by my several masters whom I have served, yet my long experience and close observation has convinced me that these three confederate kings of Sodom have, somehow or another, contrived to get back upon the earth under the modern titles of Seductionists, Compromisers and Fusionists, and that this day, in the noonday of the nineteenth century, they are leading into vile captivity, from the church and the world, tens of thousands of the race This will be the case most assuredly, unless Michael, whom John saw on the white horse, who "in righteousness judgeth and maketh war," shall lead on his illustrious troops, who are also mounted upon white horses and clothed in fine linen. I say that, unless, like Abraham of old, these troops shall recapture such enslaved souls, they will, ere long, find a very smooth, genteel and slippery gate to everlasting misery.

I saw, reader, that you looked a little cross-eyed when I spoke of Abraham's religion not taking the fight out of him. Let me say here to you, that you may compound all the graces, celestial and terrestial, that adorn angels or men, and that the single grace of love has more war and fight in it than all the rest put together. In fact, love is the pluck of them all.—Whatever love loves, it will fight for if in danger. We ask you what made the old patriots of the Revolution bare their naked bosoms to all the bullets of Great Britain? What made them fight as they did? We answer, it was love; the love of liberty. They loved it better than their lives, their property and their sacred honor.

I recollect hearing one of my associates say, while in the scavenger's rag bag; and who was formerly a part of a night gown, owned by a lady who lived in a log cabin, surrounded by hostile savages; that once in the absence of her husband a bloody fingered savage broke open the door of her cabin at midnight, seized her babe which was laying in her bosom, and endeavored to invade the precints of her virtue; but the love of purity and fidelity to her husband and love to her babe burst forth like a volcano; although, naturally timid as a fawn, yet she seized her husbands broad axe and with a single blow literally split the Indian in twain.

This is what love will do to secure the object of its desire, and a religion that will not wield spiritual weapons, and "fight the good fight of faith," not only in maintaining the honor of the "stars and stripes," as well as the standard of him, who "judgeth and maketh war;" whose vesture is dipped in blood; we say without hesitation that such a man's religion or patriotism is vain. It is unlike him who trod the wine press alone—who bared his immaculate bosom to gather all the darts of earth and hell, who hung three dreadful hours on the tree, facing the hot shot and bomb-shells from the mortars in Edom; declaring, as they flew thick and fast, in muttering thunders, "dying, thou shalt die." Unlike him whose name and nature is love, that withstood the cannonading of the law, from the batteries on Mount Sinai, for the love he bore wretched, fallen man.

This was the love of the true shepherd, who laid down his life for his sheep; and old Putnam like, with a torch-light of love in his hand, entered the dark den of millions of hearts, dragging the wolf out of his den, and bruising his head under his omnipotent heel.— This is the kind of fighting love will do. He that loveth will fight.

A battle is coming between the two kingdoms,
  The armies are gathering round;
The pure testimony and vile persecution
  Will come to close contest ere long;
Then gird on your armoar, ye saints of the Lord,
And he will direct you by his living word;
The pure testimony will cut like a sword.

CHAPTER TENTH.

I was tempted to make an apology to my readers, for playing by the way, in the flowery fields of love and matrimony; thus taking up nearly all the pages in the foregoing chapter.

But what is the use? We must have some nuts to crack, and once in a while a dish of strawberries and cream to serve up to our readers, or they would remove their washing and boarding to some other place. I have yet to learn of, or see the aged grandfather or grandmother, bachelor or maiden, who, from the time they leaped from their mother's lap, ever got tired of talking on the subject of courtship and marriage, or of the object of their loves.

The reason is, they are both plants of heavenly origin, and their theme is inexhaustible and ever pleasing.

But I see that my master and his associate partners and clerks have taken their seats in council, to devise ways and means for disposing of me and my chums in the sack, to the best advantage. My master is of course in the chair, he being the keystone of the arch.

The ancient Pharisees took council together, as to how they might smite the shepherd, and scatter the flock. A by-stander, if he had stood on Hebron and listened to the master as he with his disciples sat upon its green slopes telling them that he must soon go to the city of Jerusalem; be there mocked, scourged and crucified by the Scribes, Pharisees and Elders of the people; would, in amazement have exclaimed, what! go to Jerusalem among church members, among the rulers, the preachers, deacons, class-leaders, and exhorters, to suffer and be crucified? But strange as it may appear, my own experience, and the universal experience of my rag-bag companions, some of whom have had large ranges of observation, is, that Christ and his cause have suffered more at Jerusalem, ten times over, than among all the gentile nations combined, and this, too, from those who ruled and governed the church by the cursed principles of fusion and compromise with "the world, the flesh and the devil."—But I must listen and take down in short hand the proceedings of this secret conclave.

Little do they realize how many eyes and ears are

open about them, or tell tale children that will hereafter drag their iniquities into the light. Imprimus, I would say, that my master and partners, as St. James says, "seemed to be very religious." I have never heard of their casting out devils, but they often ate and drank at the celebration of the passover; have done many wonderful works, e. g., heading subscriptions for high steeples, frescoing Grecian marble pulpits, ministers' salaries, thundering organs, and to pay enough for grinding out music, and calling it praise to God; as also other machinery employed as a substitution for, and improvement upon spiritual worship. Then there were the grab-bags and other expenses for the support of the gospel, toward which the owners of the Pemberton mills were no small contributors.

"You see, gentlemen," said Mr. Chairman, "to what a towering height the Pemberton mills have arisen, and to what length and breadth, o'er land and sea, the odor of our name is spread. This kind of talk, however, is confined to our ears; but money is money, and glory is glory, and you know we all love it. We love to drink it in at our ears, eyes and mouth. How we can soar, and mount, and fly like the eagle; on such golden pinions and look down upon all the lesser fowls who vainly strive to rise.

The principal feathers in our wings sprang forth at the first discovery of coloring cotton warp and woolen woof in the same dye, taking special care to comb the wool over the eyes of the cotton, and also over those of purchasers, marking in large letters of gold, "Pure Saxony," and thus invoicing and selling, we have prospered."

At this point, the conscience of one of the junior partners began to rub its eyes, wake up, and to raise the query, "Who is to father the millions of lies that are told over the counter of the retailer, who swears that these goods are all wool?" At this question my master senior ran his fingers through his silver-gray fleece, walked backwards and forwards, then turning to his audience, he said, "Dear brethren, this question with me has been settled for years, and it is surprising to me that my intelligent brethren of the various denominations in Lawrence should be ignorant of the Scriptures. Has not Providence and nature, from all eternity, made the firm decree that every father is held responsible for the support and acts of his own offspring? I need not tell you, gentlemen, at this enlightened age of the world, who the father of lies is, for yourselves know him full well; and if he is the father of all lies, these brats that your consciences are so much troubled about are his legitimate children, and in spite of the old fellow, he must father them and be responsible for their tricks, and I assure you I do not intend to stand as their sponsor or God-father."

This seemed to be a very satisfactory exposition of the case, and all their consciences curled down and were very soon in a sound slumber.

"Gentlemen," again he said, "you may prepare your minds for a startling fact which I am about to relate. It will be to you as a heavy peal of thunder from the azure vault of heaven. My extensive tour among our old customers has satisfied me that all compromising platforms are to be swept by this cursed abolition deluge that is overflowing church and state all over the land, into the valley of Gehenna. As it was in the days of Noah, so now; there will not be left a plank upon which the peaceful dove may rest its feet; at least, such is the present prospect. What I mean by compromise, gentlemen, in our business, is the forming our webs with a thread of cotton and a thread of wool. It is our glorious expediency for raising funds for the support of the Gospel, rearing the Pemberton Mills to the skies, and spreading the savor of our names, as have the Rothschilds, o'er land and o'er sea. I am sorry to inform you that this 'expediency' has come to an end, and that the very best feathers we have in our extensive wings have been awfully singed. Furthermore, unless some other expediency is resorted to, the founders of Pemberton Mills, and the glory of each of our respective churches in Lawrence will surely come to the groveling plane of many of our poor neighbors. You have been expressly informed of the sad fate of one of our customers, who, attired in shirt and drawers of compromise goods, lodging in the third story of a building which caught fire, was burned up, while his companion, who was clad in shirt and drawers of woolen, was saved. This fact has awakened suspicion among all our customers, and now, every pair of breeches that is bought or sold must be run into the blaze of the candle or match, and the cotton, like compromising Christians and politicians, will always kick, and flounce, and squirm, as if it were possessed of seven devils, when persecution, with its fires, begins to rage, and thus their hypocrisy is made manifest.

But beloved, I am now about to turn your sadness into gladness. "Expediency," both in church and State, you know, is now the watchword of the present day; and I have hit upon a plan which will place new plumage on our wings: a plan too, that will puzzle the devil himself to clearly recognize, as the deception is in the web over his own children, when he sees them in church or State.

It, gentlemen, is the fusion doctrine; it is what the doctors would call the "sine qua non" for the times.—It is the quick-silver given to the despairing, dying patient; it is sure to kill or cure. My plan is as follows: that instead of cotton warp and woolen woof, to divide the cotton and wool into about equal parts, then run them several times through the pickers together, until they are perfectly "fused." Thus bury them together in the dye-kettle with the same baptism, while we gentlemen and our customers are of the same faith and of one accord. Your woof and your web will also be the same; give it a glossy exterior, a large Golden Label "Pure Saxony," and the palms of victory will be ours.

To establish this fact, gentlemen, of this "fusion" doctrine, we have only to read the history of the "Presidential Campaign" of 1860. Had the "fusion ticket" of Breckenridge, Bell and Douglas been successful, although their principles were as unlike as cotton and wool, yet the success of that fusion ticket would have hung the two keys upon the girdle of the secessionists, and the glorious institution of slavery would have sprung up and spread all over the land, and auction sales of living "Hams" would have taken place on every block from Maine to Georgia, and Abraham would have continued his rail-splitting. "Our goverment," said he, "both civil and ecclesiastical, prospered for many years "like a green bay tree," as did also our glorious Pemberton Mills, under the doctrine of compromise, when we gave the south a thousand hounds to hunt and bring their "Hams." They in return gave us a large slice from their best loaf. We had peace in all our political borders, and until

Michael's embassadors entered the temples of our fair Zion with their Abolition and Temperance scourges, twisted together, and began to upset the tables of the money changers, and the seats of them who sold negroes; we had great peace in Zion; but now we have uproar and confusion.

There is one principle more gentlemen, that you will suffer me to present before your minds, before I sit down, as proof of the successful operation of the fusion doctrine, which we are now about to adopt, which defies detection.

I speak now of the fusion of blood that courses its way through the veins of many of the sons of Ham. So completely mixed is it, that it would puzzle the slave-holder, or old father Ham himself, if he were alive, to detect, or separate his own children; and to conclude, we will risk detection, and the success of our web on the fusion doctrine."

The meeting then broke up; and we, like the goats and the sheep were parceled off, right and left. It was my good fortune to be made into a web of shirting, some of my neighbors to be transformed into all wool, other portions into ladies' dresses, such as calicoes, delaines, shallys, &c., and after going through a terrible scratching and twisting, and all manner of persecutions, we soon found ourselves back again to the great auction room in New York, neatly cared for, in webs of every description, prepared for the country merchant.

Now, therefore, when we were stored away in the steamer and all hands snoozing, I gave myself to serious reflection, something like Dr. Young's "Night Thoughts." I, of course, cast a retrospective eye over the scenes of which I was an eye-witness, in and about the region of Pemberton Mills, and more especially to analyze the "fusion doctrine" resorted to by my last master as an "expediency," as he termed it, to raise the wind, support the gospel, augment his gains, and to snuff himself the glorious odor of becoming a millionaire. While contemplating these things, awful convictions flashed upon my brain, and settled my mind that compromise and fusion were the Beelzebub sins of the day. It was the Gog and Magog, both in church and State, coming upon the breadth of the earth, encompassing our beloved Zion, and also about our beloved metropolis.

Carnal and spiritual weapons are crossing each other on the civil and ecclesiastical battle-field this day, and it might be said, Woe unto the inhabitants of America, for the old secessionist and his followers are in battle array against you. But as long as I see the keys hanging from the golden girdle of Michael, I don't believe a hair of his soldiers' heads will smell of fire. And in State, while the keys hang upon the girdle of our political Abraham, the stars and stripes will float in the pure breath of freedom.

And now, as we are about to exchange masters, we must bring this chapter to a close. I have made free use of the cotton and the wool to illustrate the political and religious sins of the day. While it is to be deprecated and condemned by all honest men, I refer to the legalized cheating by this adulterous nation in the manufacture of cloth, the poison stuffs used in the adulteration of the pure juice of the grape and in the usually termed spirituous liquors, bringing premature death to the victims and cheating the world with their mixed merchandise. Add to these the lies under which men hide themselves; these alone are enough to sink a nation. But they are winked at, and low bows made to their propagators as they sweep our sidewalks, and some of them the broad aisle of the church, arrayed in their purple and fine linen. Such men will find in the day of judgment that they will be compelled to father their own lies, and as I have looked upon the different churches, and especially when I was warming the back of my blind master, I have thought that it would puzzle the devil himself to recognize his own children, as much as to tell by their actions and life who were church members, in consequence of the fusion of the church and the world, as the church looks like a great flower-bed — a jeweler's traveling advertisement.

But I will be comforted, for Michael's sheep are all marked and on record, and "not one of them shall perish, neither shall any one pluck them out of the Father's hands."

MY FOURTH MASTER.

CHAPTER ELEVENTH.

At this point we give the parting hand to our third master, whose prominent sins were compromise and fusion. What the success of his new fusion is, we shall probably learn at the paper mill, or at the great burning day, when "every man will be judged according to his works." And now, as we have taken lodgings at the great auction mart in New York, each of us must look for a new master. Heaven alone can judge of the intense interest felt by the inmates of the coffles at a slave auction, as a hundred "land sharks" gather around the block with their gang-chains and fetters, not knowing into whose hands they shall fall. It was something so with us. We knew the hour had come when must, like sheep be scattered, every one to his own. But there was one consolation: there was not only a time to be scattered, but also a time to be gathered in. There would be a day of resurrection both of rags and slaves; one at the paper mill and the other at the "general assembly of the church of the first born, whose names are written in heaven," where loved ones meet to part no more, to tell their sufferings and shout their victories. This is the hope that keeps the heart whole. But I see that the crimson flag is flying over our door, and country merchants, from greenhorn clerks just starting business, to the silver-gray and snow white locks, are crowding eagerly around the block.

Our old probang preacher, from the cotton-fields, has taken the form, given us a few heavy raps with his hammer, opened his bull-frog mouth, and showers of smart sayings, mingled with tobacco spittle, begin to fall upon the audience, and the sales begin. I was borne off, together with some Merrimac and fusion cloth, by a dignified silver-gray dealer by retail, who lived in a beautiful country village, in the centre of the State of New York. I was marked with a good round profit from cost, and laid in a very conspicuous place on my new master's shelf, with some other shirtings, where I could both see and hear everything that was going on about the store, on both sides of the counter.

Before I advance any farther, I give it as my opinion that you may throw the net around a thousand country merchants and you will have a better haul of fish than from any puddle of pollywogs in which the human family may be gathered. They are, as a class, respectable and useful in society—true gentlemen, and some of them honest Christians.

But the object of my book is not to eulogize goodness, for that seldom ever hides itself. My contract with my publisher is, to drag secret sins from their dark dens, and expose them in the light, especially that class of sins which are so fashionable, and so palatable both in church and State. To be sure this is dirty work, to sweep from under the bed, and behind the door; and to hunt up all the spiders' nests in the dark corners of the building. I am sure no one covets my appointment by the bishop; but the servant is not greater than his lord, and Uncle Sam said, "that Massa Jesus made himself of no reputation, in consequence of doing the dirty work of house cleaning."

Human bodies in the bible are called houses; and the class of people whose occupation it is to go from house to house in the city, begging the privilege of cleaning filthy houses and sweeping chimnies, are considered among the lowest class of kitchen furniture, or servants; and in this place we are startled at the infinite stoop of the "Prince of the kings of the earth," in knocking at every sinner's door, saying, "wilt thou be cleansed from thy filthiness?" Yes, he has stood knocking until his locks have become wet with the dews of the night, with the pardoning blood and cleansing water, begging to enter into the very Synagogue of satan, bind the strong man, cast him out, cleanse the house, garnish the walls, and then come himself, and bring his father, who will spread the banquet of love, dwell in the holy temple, and ultimately exalt him to a seat among the honorable on his throne. But alas! how many of us are locking out our best friend.

One of the prominent and fashionable sins of my new master was "expedient lying." This was common currency which at par passed freely on the counter, between merchant and customer, and this sin has been one of so long standing, and so fashionable among both professors and the world, that conscience is wearied out with rebuking, and with eyes red with weeping has fallen into a sound sleep. This habit, by its longevity, has become as grey as the head of my new master. Doubtless he will entail this legacy upon his clerks, to whom it will be said "as your father did, so do ye."

I will give you an illustration of this expedient falsehood. An old customer came and enquired for a coat's cloth pattern; my venerable master, and by the way I had forgotten to tell you he was a professor of religion, brought forth a roll of "Fusion Saxony cloth," displayed to his customer the beauty of its texture, and said, "this, my brother, is none of your compromising stuff, that powder mill is blown up." After the customer had enquired the price, my master then looked at his private mark, slipped his fingers through his silver grey locks, and looking his customer in the face, while a smile overspread his features, said: "As you are an old friend and customer, you shall have a coat from that cloth at about cost;" you shall have that piece of cloth for four dollars a yard, and," said he, slapping his hand upon the counter, "that is about what it cost." The bargain was struck, his customer returned home greatly consoled, not only with the purity and cheapness of the cloth, but also with the exhibition of kindness, which, like water, flowed from the merchant's heart. His son, who then stood at his elbow, speaking in a low tone, said "father, I suppose you know that you sold that cloth for just double what it cost; how then can you reconcile your conscience, declaring to your friend that you sold it to him at about cost."

"Ah, my son," said the old man, "I see you are yet a novice in the trade, and have not become familiar with the expediency; I told our customer no lie; you remember John, that I said *about cost;* this is an indispensable word, and most successfully used by all retailers, in fact, of every trade. You know your grandfather in turning about his team, can sweep about as large a circle as may suit his convenience. So also, the word "about" is so elastic that you can stretch it to any extent, without awakening conscience, or telling a lie. It is a license of so long a standing, granted by expediency.

And thus the father entailed this legacy upon his son, who became his lawful heir, and he no doubt will entail it to the latest generation.

Now my master, on any other occasion, would not tell a bare-faced falsehood to save his life, and I never knew him to ask God to forgive him for one of these elastic whoppers. If I had been made with nerves I should have squirmed off the shelf while hearing the common place lying which took place at my master's counter, while the work of "Jewing down" was going on. I believe I shall not tell any thing about the clerks making "small drafts upon the tiller" about the time there was to be a star player on the boards of the opera, or a little previous to a "fuddle." Their wages were small, and their demands were peremptory; and expediency came to their relief, and "like master, like man," stultified their little tender conscience, and all was made right, as this account was never reckoned in as loss or gain.

There is another brood of liars I believe I must speak of, while I have the rascal by the ear, lest at any time I should let them slip. I am almost afraid I shall offend my reader by christening these children by such a hard name. They are most of them children of the blood royals of the day, little harmless deceivers, is the softest name I can call them.

When I see an old bachelor in pulpit or pew with a youthful fleece, resting upon his wrinkled brow, thinks I to myself, that's a lie. When I see an aged matron or maiden, with her head adorned with glossy raven locks gracefully dangling by the side of her rose and lily cheeks, or hanging in curls over a swan-like neck of sweet seventeen, I set them down as two more lies, or as little painted, mischievous deceivers. When I see deformity made perfectly symmetrical, thinks I to myself, there's a little cotton padding not a mile off; but these are fashionable, genteel, and some folks think harmless.

Well, reader, I see that you are staring me in the face, half inclined to kick the author, and throw his book into the fire, for intermeddling with such little harmless household and family matters. Tell me, says the nervous reader, what harm they have ever done, and why these children should be classed, or christen ed after the naughty name of deceivers, which means nothing less than square up and down, plumpers."

Well, in the first place they are hypocrites, painted sepulchres, which indeed outwardly appear beautiful to the superficial observation of men. But strip the dye stuff from the youthful fleece of the bachelor and you will find the sear and yellow leaf of longevity; remove the glossy and raven rocks and ringlets from the aged matron and maiden, and the removal will reveal the silver grey, and the furrows of age ; remove the artificial rose and lily from the maiden's cheek, and you will discover the tracks of the pale horse and his rider.

I am hereby reminded of a story that was told me by one of my companions, that perchanced to lodge one night with me in the scavenger's rag bag. I discovered that he was the leg of a pair of drawers; and before we fell asleep I enquired of him whose limbs he had clothed in the past; for I must confess that my bedfellow, from the filth he brought in with him, was rather a suspicious bed fellow.

He said his master was a very wealthy and miserly old bachelor, who succeeded in winning the hand of a very fair and rosy cheeked damsel of the village. They both agreed to take the emigrant train together, which carried passengers from the barren country of celibacy and let them down in the flowery and fertile fields, in the state of matrimony; or rather, as I thought, instead of matrimony, a matter-of-money.

Well, to make the story short, about the wedding, the bridal chamber was beautifully adorned and illuminated, and the youthful bride after being snugly nightcapped, &c., her waiting maids left the room. My master who was the bridegroom as he stood by the side of the fair one while cementing was going on under the direction of a clergyman; gave the appearance of one who had shed his milk teeth and just arrived at the stature of a perfect man, with a beautiful fleece of auburn hair, form symmetrical, in short, a perfect model of a youthful bridegroom. But when, in process of time, he entered the chamber where the single dove lay in the nest, he, after laying off some of his outer habiliments, proceeded to take off his auburn wig, which left him, like a sloop which, by the winds, had been stripped of all its sails, to "scud under a bare poll." He then took out a beautiful glass eye and laid it upon the stand; and after he had drawn a few pounds of cotton, which had assisted nature in her handiwork, filling up valleys, &c., from his limbs, he began to unscrew a cork leg. At this juncture of the case, the dove left her nest as suddenly as if a hawk had been whetting up his talons, and eloped.

"Oh, mother," said she, "I thought I had married a man, but he is made up of false hair, glass eyes, paint, cork, straps, and all such things. He has taken himself all to pieces."

Now I will ask you, reader, was there ever a greater lie told, and that, too, by these harmless, speechless brood of deceivers?

But before I close this chapter, I must relieve myself of one more of the secret sins of this cheating brood; and that you may understand me fully, you will suffer me to relate a short story which was related to me by a piece of fine linen, which had served as a shirt collar to one of the wealthy lords in her Majesty's dominions. He said his master, having several tenants of the common peasantry, one of whom had been sick for some years, until he was not able to pay his rent, his master at once served up a writ of ejectment, which turned him and his defenceless household into the street. This procedure awakened sympathy for the oppressed and indignation for the oppressor among the neighbors. "It so happened," said he, "as my master came strutting along the sidewalk like a tom-turkey in the barnyard, that one of his neighbors saluted him thus: 'I understand, 'squire, that you have had several letters, or writs of ejectment; that you are soon to be turned out of your marble front palace, as well as to leave the whole plantation, and I understand that the ejectment is in consequence of old debts brought up against you.'

At this state of the case, my master turned around, and, looking as red as a turkey's comb, said, as he swore vehemently and struck down his gold-headed cane upon the pavement, 'I owe no debts; I have never had a writ of ejectment served upon me, or a letter to leave my mansion.' His neighbor then very significantly pointed to the white hairs in his fleece. 'What are these,' said he, 'but a thousand letters to warn you that your time is short, and that you are about to leave your stately mansion for the narrow house in the silent tomb? Death has an old demand against you, which must soon be paid. The grave-worm also has a demand upon your pampered body which must be gratified.'"

And now comes the application. Has not a merciful Providence placed upon us gray hairs, pale cheeks, dilapidated frames, nervous debilities — every one of them letters, legibly written, that the time of our departure is at hand? Do they not say, "Be ye also ready?" And shall we, in order to deceive ourselves, besmear these letters with dye-stuffs and paints, and then stand before our mirrors with a flattering tongue, more than half making us believe we are yet in the vigor of youth, and thereby filling up or concealing our new dug grave, or shoving it many years in the future?

These, with many others, are among the deceptive and fashionable sins of the day, both in church and State.

CHAPTER TWELFTH.

In the latter part of the last chapter I "switched off" a little from the main track, as touching the things directly relating to the secret sins of my present master, who, in addition to his mercantile business and church fellowship, was also a member in the highest initiatory orders of our secret conclaves, viz: the Masonic and Odd Fellow fraternities. I have, I think, on the outset, called them by their proper names, secret sins, and, as a cast-off rag, I am glad to feel that my opinion is not "the end of the law for righteousness," so far as they are concerned, as I never was inside of one of their lodges. As heretofore, what I shall have to say will be what I have heard; but nevertheless, if my master is associated with any institution whose doings he is not willing should be turned inside out, I, with my generous judgment, will pronounce it as far from the Gospel institution as a pigeon could fly in a month. But just at this time there is a good spirit whispering in my interior ear, advising me to skip over these Siamese twins, fearing they might bring down an avalanche of wrath, and I should be thrown from the shelves, and book and author kicked into the street as a miserable tell-tale and disturber of the peace. But I have an adage which I clap on to every thing; even the family converse between the husband and wife, the soul and its God, and that is this: "Pure gold never loses anything by being revealed, even when passing through the crucible of the outside world." I think that the Abrahamic Cabinet ought to tell all its doings to every body, even if the secessionists do profit by it. Oh, I do hate anything secret. Boards and walls ought to be transparent, and no family whose doings are justifiable ought to have window curtains, and all apparel and pockets ought to be made of gauze, so that the innocence of our hearts and doings might be made manifest to all, and so all should approve our freedom from guile and all hypocrisy.—A declaration was made eighteen hundred years ago, by one to whom every secret thing is manifest, forever settling one fact, that there was a class of people who always love darkness, giving as a reason, because their deeds are evil. While on the other hand, honest men and women always love the light; in fact, they love to be searched out with a candle.

If there had been no sheep-stealing wolf in the den, old Putnam would have returned and reported that there was no thief there; but when the people did drag him out, they also drew out a wolf with him. And so let it be with our investigations to-day in search of these secret wolves in these dens of deep obscurity where window-curtained families reside. But a maiden lady at my right hand has suggested that this open gauze work would do if all people were blind, but the fact that so many folks like obscurity is to me a proof that the world is full of wickedness. In my opinion, open daylight should be practiced.

But I see that there has a venerable white-locked pilgrim entered the store. Old Jacob-like, he is leaning upon his staff. It was a gloomy day. The rain was fast falling, the clerks and customers were all absent, and none left but the solitary trio, this old weeping Jeremiah, my master and myself. After the usual salutation, the old pilgrim, with a sigh and a sepulchral groan, as if he was about to call a Lazarus from the tomb, thus addressed my master:

"I have called to-day to have a serious and friendly talk and labor of love with thee, my beloved brother, concerning your connection with Odd Fellowship and Free Masonry."

Thinks I to myself, this is a golden moment for me. This old saint is a kind of God-send, an angel standing in the sun. I therefore pricked up my ears, and in short hand, began to note down the following dialogue:

"These secret institutions," said the old man, "may or may not be good in their place; may do for worldly minds, that are strangers to higher and holier things; but you my, brother and son in the gospel, have long since professed to haul down the flag of the prince of this world, and to have run up upon your halyards the flag of the Prince of Peace, with its "lone star." You have at the baptismal waters called heaven and earth to witness that you had forever separated yourself from all vanities and vain glories. As a chaste virgin you have sworn eternal fidelity to Jesus Christ, as your husband." At this my master's chin began to quiver, with guilt, anger or shame, or all combined, I know not, but his face was as red as a turkey's comb, and goatee; then slapping his fist down upon the counter, as much as to say, I have a knock-down argument, old daddy, which will lay you flat on the floor, he said: "Do you think that our minister, who has graced our pulpit from sabbath to sabbath, together with a batalion of pious and *prominent* clergy, which belong to our denomination, and other evangelical bodies of christians, would belong to any institutions which were not heaven born and heaven bound? Do you think that such men would sail in daylight on the old ship Zion, and under the clouds of night steal away from their families, and all outsiders to embark on a piratical craft? Is it any more wrong" said my master, "for men to meet during the evening to work out their purposes of benevolence with mankind, than to be employed till a late hour of the night, night after night, at the expense of their business, at "protracted meetings," in severe danger of losing their health, and incurring the penalty of Bronchitis?

"These men," said he, "can tower to the clouds with their eloquence and logic, and bring down thunder, lightning, &c.; go first and labor with them, before you come to angle for the small fish. It's enough for me to follow my preacher or class leader; as Paul said, 'be ye followers of me!'"

My master then folded up his arms, crossed his legs, threw out his cardamon buds, and began to breath freely. He then took a cigar from his case, and offering one to his old friend, which was refused, began to puff and smoke like a propeller.

The look of my master was as much as to say, "I have now spiked your cannon old fellow, you may as well return home, say your prayers, and at your time of life not be meddling with institutions, the character of which you do not understand."

Reader, if you have ever beheld the king of day, in a fair May morning, rising out of a calm sea of glass, gilding the iron pillar of Peter the Great, you have some idea of the firmness, serenity, and calm sunshine which now fell from the wrinkled face of the old man upon my master. "My dear brother," said he, "while attentively listening to your arguments, which I will not pretend to say, are without some plausibility, yet you know that a keen-eyed trout will not bite a false fly, though it may appear to be genuine. The deceiver can transform himself into an angel of light, into any thing but an angel of love, and if he deceived your mother, no marvel much more her degenerate children. You have doubtless read in the "Pilgrim's Progress" how Christiana and her children came near being poisoned to death, in consequence of plucking fruit from the branches of Beelzebub's orchard, that hung so gracefully over the walls into the king's highway, ravishing to the eye, and luscious to the flesh, equal to that which your mother was forbidden to eat, and in consequence of which the crown fell from her head, and she sickened and died beneath its ravishing boughs, proffering the same deadly fruit to the lips of her husband and Lord; and it was thus the fountains were poisoned, and new graves were dug amidst the bowers of Eden.

Christiana chided her children, as I shall you, for their want of carefulness and watchfulness. "Why, mother," said they, "have not all the pilgrims and the children a perfect right to all the fruit in the king's highway?" "Most assuredly, my loves," replied Christiana, "but before you pluck this fruit you must first cast your eyes to the root of the tree and see whose ground it springs from." He who cast up this highway for pilgrims, suffers these branches to be extended over the walls in order to test the fidelity and obedience of his children, all of which they are forbidden to touch on any pretense. It is so with the branches which spring forth from these worldly institutions, these Secret Societies.

They extend all over Immanuel's ground, and under their branches lie the bleached bones of thousands of the embassadors of the Lord Jesus Christ, and many more of their flocks, whose carcasses have fallen in the wilderness.

"Every tree is known by its fruit." The fairest apple on this tree, and the most seductive fruit is named, I believe, "christian benevolence." Let us examine this tree before us:

I would enquire, is it any thing more than a "Mutual Insurance Company?" These will not insure a house contiguous to a powder mill, because it would be the surety of having to pay, and perhaps speedily the total of the sum guaranteed in the policy of insurance.

I see that a Life Insurance Agent is seated in his office, leaning his elbow on a package of life policies. Then enters a healthy and robust young man with fifty or one hundred dollars in his hand; he wants his life insured. He casts his money into the treasury, and is at once insured.

There is little or no danger of his speedy death, and they feel safe. Were the risk prominent, he would be obliged to pay a large sum in addition, or be rejected.

It is so, I suppose, with Odd Fellowship and Free Masonry. A rap is heard at the door of their Lodges.

If the applicant is young, healthy and sound, and his hands full of money, the black cap is drawn over his eyes, and he is led into the wonderful secret, and gets, as he thinks, the worth of his money.

I now see coming a poor man, with patches on his knees, emaciated form, and pennyless. He raps timidly at the door, tells the porter, who stands there with a drawn sword or other deadly weapon, all his sorrows; how that his wife and children have been sick, and were then suffering for bread; and that these institutions were conducted for charitable purposes. He is then told that these doors of mercy could not be opened to beggars, nor those who had infirmities about them, as thereby no funds could be raised to carry out their charitable purposes; that the most of their money was expended to buy Regalias, wine and other refreshments after lodge hours; and that if any was left it was expended in burying the dead with pompous displays, and decorating the lodge rooms.

I saw my master began to squirm as if he were sitting on nettles. "Hold a moment," said the old man, "let me compare this fruit with that which grows on the tree of life. Did Jesus Christ ever reject a beggar that made a draft on his charity? No, never. But he did reject the rich and proud Pharisee, clad in purple and fine linen, while in his omnibus of free grace,

'The poor, the maimed, the halt, the blind,
In him a hearty welcome find.'

Did Jesus Christ enter into some secret conclave in order to perform his acts of benevolence? Oh, no. All his acts and charities were swung out in mid-heaven, like the sun, where all could gaze upon it, be cheered with its rays and warmed by its golden beams. Allow me to hold you by the skirt," said the old man, "a little longer, my dear brother. As you referred to the Apostle Paul, who said, "Be ye followers of me," consider his teachings in another place also. He told the Corinthians that the offering of a good piece of beefsteak to a dumb idol did not poison the beef or impregnate it with idolatry. Nevertheless, if they, by eating meat thus offered to idols, should in any way grieve, offend, or cause to offend any of the weak brethren or sisters in the church or out of it, that he, for one, would always deny himself the luxury. My dear brother," continued he, "I now speak, as I believe, in the fear of God. I do believe that if you could gather up all the tears which have been shed by church members, and add to them the tears of the wives of Odd Fellows and Masons, which have been shed over these two institutions, they would float the Great Eastern. Many do believe, whether it be true or not, that there is death in the pot, that none of this fruit is ever gathered from the boughs of Paradise unless it be from the one that was forbidden by the sovereign of the skies, under whose boughs lay the bleached bones of poor sinners, as seen in Ezekiel's visions.

"One more plank," said the old man, "of your platform, let me examine, and one upon which you appear to stand so firmly, and then, positively, I will bid you good night. It is the plank you make of ministers of the Gospel. They seem to brood all the lesser chickens under their wings. Suffer me, by way of comparison, to place another plank alongside of yours, which, according to my logic, will be composed of about the same kind of timber. I will now throw the net around a thousand ministers South of Mason and Dixon's line, and bid them stand on this plank. Where, among the sons of men, will you find a more brilliant, intellectual, and profound class of men than these very gentlemen? They tell their audiences, as they stand behind an open Bible, that HUMAN SLAVERY, also, is a HEAVEN-BORN INSTITUTION. They will open the graves, also, of their fore-fathers, who were buried in their Masonic regalia, and call up their spirits, and tell you that from those blessed lips they were taught the doctrine of the glorious institution of chattel slavery. Do you think they will ask if such Doctors of Divinity are not now walking with the patriarchs and prophets on the plains of the heavenly Dura?"

The old man, with his cheeks bathed in tears, then stretched forth his hand to my master, and bade him an affectionate farewell. He then walked out as nimbly as a youth, feeling that he had rolled his heavy burden from his own shoulders upon those broad shoulders of my master, who now seemed to have the greatest difficulty in keeping the last plank of his platform beneath his feet.

CHAPTER THIRTEENTH.

My Dear Reader: You have seemed to listen with some interest as I have narrated, or, as some would say, sanctioned, the roasting of my master upon the gridiron. But as the Dutchman told the Irishman, as they stood together upon the fatal platform, "Hanging," said he, "ish noting for you, 'cause all your nation got used to it." If all stories are true, the gridiron is a piece of kitchen furniture used in all these lodges with which my master is familiar. If it could speak, it might tell us of the numerous hams which have been broiled upon its heated bars. But then this is all outside talk, and perhaps some of my rag companions which have been used for the purpose of enveloping hams from the impudent house flies could give us more light on the subject, if any one had the curiosity to discover the secret.

I did think I would shut down the gate, in the foregoing chapter, touching the secret and fashionable sins of the day, and which were practiced by my master; but if you knew, dear reader, how uneasy an untold secret makes me, you would allow me to empty my satchel. I have already served seven masters, and my last sad office was to poultice the shins of a very son of Bacchus, from whence I took lodgings in the scavenger's rag-bag, from which place I now dictate the things relating to my own experience. It so happened on a time that the subject of secret societies was the topic of conversation among my chums in the same bag, and we had a kind of Methodist love-feast; or, I should have said, this was the order of the meeting. Each rag stood in its place and related its experience in what it had seen and heard touching the subject which is now before us. It is a proverb among Methodists, and, indeed, is incorporated as one of their fundamental doctrines, that "No one really knows anything except what is known by heartfelt experience," especially on the subject of religion. Certainly, every witness destitute of this personal experience or knowledge would be rejected by the judge in any court, whether in heaven or on the earth. The Devil and his followers care but little about the eloquence of the lawyer, if they can only manage to seal the lips of the faithful and honest witness. But we must listen to the evidence, as I see there is one of the audience on the block of testimony. He proceeded to state that it fell to his lot to do the dirty work of a pocket handkerchief for a rather wild young man, living in a small village a little east of Utica.

"I think," said he, "it was in the year 1824. The young man, I understand, after I was cast into the rag-bag, went into the Southern States and engaged extensively in business, and finally became blind. But what I am about to say upon this subject is as follows: There lived in that village, or walked about in that village, one of the most bloated of the sons of Bacchus. He was in fellowship with the lodge of Masons in that place. His head was swollen like a pumpkin, his eyes were bound around with the coarsest kind of red ferreting, his nose resembled, in appearance, a dead ripe strawberry of the largest variety, and, to cap the crimes of life, this once husband and father was driven by the devils of delirium tremens, a mass of corruption, into the narrow house. He was enough to turn the stomach of anything, except that of a Southern turkey buzzard, or, milder name, a grave worm. Well, as it came to pass, this man, I am sorry to say, was buried with all the honors, pomp and display that the brethren of the order could lavish over his remains. This was many years ago, when drinking was not considered so dire a disgrace as at present; but time can never efface from my memory that death nor the funeral obsequies.

And what a procession after such a bloat! There were probably a hundred men, among whom were ministers, and members of various religious denominations, members of the bar, thickly intermingled with drunkards, libertines and infidels; the whole company flapped, or rather aproned, on some of which were stamped various devices, their meaning known, I suppose, by the wearer; on some of their heads was a tall cap of tin or pasteboard, on which was inscribed in blazing capitals "Holiness to the Lord." There was one who was a familiar acquaintance of mine, who, I should judge from his scarlet sash, and badges tastefully arranged on his person, was clothed with power and clad with the glory of the institution, and although he also had inscribed upon his cap "Holiness to the Lord," I knew him to be a blasphemer and libertine. But to cap the climax as the procession moved toward the grave, a grey-headed infidel and drunkard marched in front with a large open bible, swung on a sash before him, with a pair of spectacles lying on its sacred pages. Unconverted as I was, thinks I, there goes a precious jewel hung on the snout of a swine. These things, together with the sermon preaching him into heaven, whether by a Universalist preacher or not, I know not; the telling the mourners that their loss was his gain, and forty other things disgusted and forever sickened me of the glories of all such institutions.

After this witness took his seat, there came on the stand a rag of fine, cleanly white muslin. "I, said he," was for several years a part of a white cravat, that was worn by one whom they termed an old fashioned Methodist preacher, of the Black River Conference, New York. He was then one of the fathers and patriarchs of that body, and I am strongly tempted to tell his name. It was Rev. ———, but I forbear.

A conference session of that body was convened, in about the year 1850. This subject was propounded in open Conference.

"What shall be done with our young preachers, who are connecting themselves with secret societies, and thereby rendering themselves odious and offensive to a large majority of their congregations, who under the discipline are obliged to accept of them, or none?"

The venerable Bishop declared that there was no discipline which directly referred to their cases; but as a father advised them to come out from among them. At this point my master arose in his seat, and as I happened to be one of the long ends which hung down upon his vest, I could plainly see the tears which floated in his dark blue eyes, and soon began to overflow the furrows in his care-worn cheek.

After blowing and choking a while he arranged his

speaking oracle, and said: "My beloved sons in the gospel; before I fall asleep in Jesus, suffer me to warn you to abstain from these institutions, which, to say the least, have the appearance of evil among the most of our pecple. When I first began to preach, it was like a perfect pump, whose pipe and valves were submerged in a well, filled with pure water. I stood before my people like a young Timothy; the very first time I bore down upon the handle the water leaped out, and the sound was coo-chug, coo-chug, like that which leaped forth from the rock, and my flocks were well watered; and the sons and daughters of Zion, like Rebecca of old after she had watered the asses of Isaac's servant, had a full pitcher to carry home to their friends. But beloved," said the old Patmos John, "I soon began to be sorely tempted, and began to dishonor God by distrusting him for my daily bread and other comforts for the body, fearing that the promises of God might fail.

There was thrown out to me on the hook of expediency the seductive bait of leaning on the sinking fund of Free Masonry; and I soon became a chaplain in the lodge, and a chum of all its members, and finally "a hail fellow, well met" at their refreshment boards, where we had crackers soaked in wine, and other liquors. My influence drew several of the male members of the flock, breaking the hearts of our wives, who could not be let into the secret, and who with sleepless eyes and half parting lips waited our midnight return; while others, without the grace of patience, like the wife of Burns, "nourished their wrath to keep it warm."

I began about this time, like many others of my brethren, to steal other preachers' sermons, bought skeleton books, enlarged the borders of my foolscap, and they were systematically and wonderfully arranged; but were as cold as a locomotive without fire or steam.

When I walked with God, and I heard the Bishop's voice, saying "whom shall we send, and who will go for us?" I, like young Isaiah, with my lips burning with seraphic fire, would respond 'Here am I, send me,' to any place or circuit where there are either saints or sinners, or both."

"But alas!" said he, "the fine gold became dim, the old church bell as it called me to the pulpit, had lost its joyful sound. I played the handle of the pump as usual, up and down very gracefully, but it rattled in the ears of the thirsty sheep like a tinkling Cymbal. My well was without water; I was, in short, a withered fig tree."

"My flock grew lean, trying to live upon bare-boned skeletons, thus things continued until a flash of lightning from Mount Sinai, made visible my darkness. I saw myself in an unjustified state, and I began to flee from the wrath to come. The elect lady being burdened for me, travailed in birth, and glory to God, I was soon delivered from this womb of darkness." At this point hearty "Amens," and shouts of "Glory to God," flew around the old church, like bursting bombs from our Spiritual Sumter, the fragments of which broke out the devil's windows in all that neighborhood."

"And now, to conclude," said my venerable master, "I will give you freely my opinion upon this subject by an illustration. It is a gray-headed, household anecdote, told on a thousand occasions to illustrate itching curiosity:

"A venerable householder," said he, "when about to take an excursion into the country, in order to prove the fidelity of his housemaid, caught a mouse and imprisoned the little quadruped by turning a wooden bowl over him on the middle of the carpeted floor in the parlor. As he was about leaving his house with his family, he handed her a bunch of keys, and said:

"Sally, with those keys you can have free access to every room and every locker in the house; but," said he, as he looked her sternly in the eye, "I charge you most emphatically not to lift up the wooden bowl that is turned over in the middle of the carpeted room."

He then entered his carriage with his wife and

children, cracked his whip, and was soon out of sight. Sally soon began to be distressed. Her curiosity was aroused like a tempest in a tea kettle.

"What do I care," said she, "for this bunch of keys that opens every door in the house? But I am distressed to know what on earth is under that wooden bowl which I am forbidden even to take a peep at."

She began to pace the room, and looked out at the windows and doors.

"Now," said she, "there is nobody coming, and I am bound — yes, I am bound, let the consequences be what they may, that my longing peepers shall be gratified."

So she laid flat upon the floor, raised the edge of the wooden bowl, and out popped the tell-tale mouse.

"Oh, dear!" said she, "is that all that is under here? Horrible disappointment! "But," said she, "I must hunt up that little four-legged slave," and she began to put in practice the fugitive slave law; but the little rogue kept his eye on the North star, and took the underground railroad.

While Sally was resolving herself into a vigilance committee, the master came home and entered the parlor, but Sally entered the closet. As soon as he had entered the room, his eye caught sight of the little capering mouse hunting for crumbs about the carpet, thus revealing the whole secret. He then cried out, as was done on a similar occasion,

'Where art thou, Sally?'

"And now, to conclude," said he, addressing the Bishop, "just turn this wooden bowl over, let out the mouse, and let Odd Fellows and Free Masons transact their business as all other benevolent societies and associate bodies do: throw open their doors and invite in wife, children and friends, both as contributors and recipients, and the whole secret of these societies would burst like a bubble into thin air."

Many other things were said by my associates in the rag-bag, touching the old Morgan affair, and of the ridiculous Tom foolery that they HEARD of. But on this subject further deponent saith not.

CHAPTER FOURTEENTH.

Once more, reader, I strive to gain your approbation. But before I draw the strings of my night-cap, suffer me to give you a small dose of cotton plantation theology. The story I have just related to you, concerning the wooden bowl and mouse, presents the picture of old days in rainbow colors before me. Although years and years have rolled away, and the hero and heroine of my tale have passed to the brighter realms of glory. yet I remember the tales which I heard in the days of my cotton-field experience. Old folks, like you and I, reader, have forgotten a thousand and one things, important things, too, which were transacted around us in middle life up to yesterday. While in dreams and visions of the day and night, it is easy to throw a summerset over half a century and strike on our feet on the play-ground of our youth.

My theologians are no one else than Uncle Sam, aided in his talk by his wife Dinah. Sam was a regular Doctor of Divinity and he learned to read the Bible, as I have told you, from his mother Eunice and grandmother Lois, early in life, before he left the hot-bed in Maryland. His eye caught the promise, "To him that overcometh will I give to drink of the water of life freely." He had, therefore, no occasion to place his clean wooden dish to catch the water that had coursed its way through a diversity of brains and human pipes, partaking and tasting sometimes of the half-rotten logs; but he dipped up his theology from the head and fountain of the spiritual Croton, as it gushed out beneath the throne of God and the Lamb. In short, he was taught of God. But let us listen to this theologian, and as he is of full age, he shall speak for himself. At the time I now refer to, there was a heavy cloud poising itself, like an eagle, over the cotton-fields of my first master, and soon began, in copious effusion, to moisten our roots and baptize Uncle Sam and Aunt Dinah, so that they dropped their hoes and took shelter under a contiguous booth, from whence I could distinctly hear the inimitable sermon.

Uncle Sam and Dinah were none of your padlock matches, but a genuine wedlock, cemented with conjugal love. Therefore they both took their seats close side by side to wait the abatement of the rain, which was now pouring in torrents. Aunt Dinah now gave Sam a hearty love-tap, slapping him on his Corderoys.

"Sam," says she, "dere is one ting, I cant get trough dis yer ole wooly head ob mine. You know Sam, I once most tink hard ob the Lor kase he make so many niggas ob us slabes, jes kase dat ar ole massa Noah when he get 'toxicated, was'nt cubber wid de blanket ob ole Ham. What little ting like dat ar make sich great fuss wid de world, an so much sorrow 'mong de slabes. But all dat be made right, kase our minister tell me, twas in de Bible so, and dat the Lor no ebry ting, an poor nigger no noting, no how. So my mine clar on dat, an ise gwine to be satisfy 'bout dat. But," says she, "dar be one ting dat 'plex dis ole head more dan forty dem ole blankets. Now Sam," says she, "while de good Lor pourin down de rain on de cotton fiel, I axes you to 'splain one ting to ole Dinah. What dat ar fruit wur, dat ole Missa Adam jes tase ob, dat rase de berry debil 'mong the niggas, white folks an all de quality, all ober de wurl ?"

Old Sam now squared himself around for the work, for like his illustrious master, he could preach with as much fervency, power and eloquence to a single woman at Jacob's well, as to a thousand. I discovered at this point the upward turned eye of this doctor of divinity, as he began to make a draft on the bank. His mighty chest began to swell as if the tide was rushing in from the ocean and swelling the banks. He then began to open his mouth which displayed two rows of well set ivory.

"Dinah," said he, "may de good Lor bress your ole heart, an mine too while we 'splain dis ere berry delicate subjec. Dar be a good many tings in de Bible dat can be 'splained to niggas, dat cant be 'splained to de white quality kase dey blush so when dey cum to de light. All dese great preachers dat got grate larnin hab grate deal to say 'bout dat ar 'bidden fruit, but none ob dem eber 'splain to de white quality what dat ar fruit wur."

"Dat ar am de trufe Sam," said Dinah, "may de good Lor help you to 'splain 't to me, so dat I ress easy on dat ar subjec."

At the conclusion of this ejaculatory prayer there was a hearty Amen from Uncle Sam, which started every bat and mole from their nests in the old shanty. All things being ready, and with the ears of his audience itching and mouth watering, the preacher began his subject:

"De berry fus ting de good Lor do," said the preacher, "was to make dis worl' out ob noting; and when he had set out all de fruit tree, an hang out de sun in de heaben, he go up on a high mountain, look all roun an say, "berry good, firs rate." Den de nex ting de Lor do, he make up a grat mortar bed, jus as you in de dough trof, do Dinah, when you is gwine to make de bread, an de pie, an de baby cake for de childer, and all such tings. De fus ting he make is an elifan, (eliphant) den he make de elifan a wife, an den de Lor marry dem, tel dem lub each odder, an hab a whole heap ob little elifan; an so de good Lor go on an make all de animals, little an big, ob de male and female. Den he marry dem, tell dem be good to each odder, an multiply, an 'plenish, an fill all de worl wid de little one. Berry well. De nex ting de good Lor do, he go down to de sea an make de big whale, den he wife, den he marry dem, an tell dem go house keeping, and hab whol heap ob little whale, an so on down to de little fish. Berry well. Den de nex ting de Lor do, he go to work an make de grat eagle, an all the ress ob de fowls dat fly in de hebens. Den he make a grat weddin for dem all, tell dem go build house, an hab heap little one too. Den he tell de ole rooster be good to de ole hen; den he tell de ole hen she mus not peck her husban. Den de Lor look roun on dem all, say, "firs rate, berry well."

At this point Aunt Dinah began to question the theology of the preacher.

"Massa Jack says," said Aunt Dinah, "dat de Lor make every ting dat hab bref, out ob de dirt, an you Sam, say dat de Lor make de fish, and fowl out ob de watta. How's dat ole feller?"

"Set down 'gain Dinah," said Sam, "I 'splain all dat ar: de Lor make de fish an fowl ob de watta, kase it be not so much hebby as de clay, so dat dey can swim in the watta, an float in de ar. Den de Lord he turn roun an say to all de animal dat he gwine to make dem a king to rul ober dem, kase de Lor hab so many odder tings to see to. Den de Lor go to work an try he bes to make a man. So he wet up some ob de finis ob de dus inter clay; an you no Dinah, dat de clean flour make aller the clean white bread. So de Lor make Adam out ob the clean dus, but arter de ole sarpent sow de tare 'mong de wheat; den ebbry body made ob de smutty flour. Den de Lor stan 'fore a grat lookin glas an see hisse'f; den he say, I make man like myse'f too. Berry well. Little whil' de Lor hab Adam made jus' like de pattern, only he not go kase he hab no life in he body."

"Jes' so," said Dinah, "jes' like ole massa's pra'r he read from de gilt edge' pra'r book ebbry Sunday; great big word, but dar be no life in dem." "Den," resumed Sam, "de Lor' git down an' he blow a little while in Adam's nose, an' when de bellers war full an' de pump 'gan to work, den de red cheek come on massa Adam. He open his eye, an' de fus' ting he see war de Lor' dat make him. As David say, he wake up an' look jes' like de Lor' hesef. Den Adam jump up, spat he han's an' say, 'Bress de Lor'. Den he look all roun', see all de nice ting de Lor' make, an' 'gin to shout, 'Glory to God.' He act jes' like all ob de Lor's convart when de Lor' breave de Holy Ghose inter dar souls. Dey open der eyes an' say, 'brees de Lor',' den look roun' an' say, 'glory to God,' an' jump up, an' spat der han's, kase dey got inter a new worl' ob light—kase dey hab 'sperience, you see, Dinah. Berry well. Purty soon de Lor' call to Adam to set down, kase he gwine to tell him someting. He war den like ebbry new born chile. He know de Lor' kase he tase ob him, an dat war good, an he know he war alibe (alive) an had his eyes open, an dat he war downright happy, an' nobody could cheat him out ob dat no how. Den de Lor' 'gan to teach him, an' tell him dat he mus' take car' an' rule ober ebbryting he make on de plantation. Den de Lor' gib massa Adam a horn an' tell him to soun' it. So Adam do as de good Lor' tell him, an' den come along de elefan' an' his wife, an' all de little elefans, an' Adam name dem all, an' so on till all de beasts an' de fowl war named. Den massa Adam get up on de stan' an' he blow de horn agin, kase dey gwine to hab de family worship. Fust ting Adam git down on his knees an' 'gin to pray. He did not hab to tell de Lor', as good many ob de 'fessors (professors) now days do, dat he war a great sinner; he sin ebbry day ob his life, an hab religion, too. Oh, no. Massa Adam hab no guilty conscience, but all he could say war, 'bress de Lor', O my soul,' dat ebbryting on de plantation praise de Lor'. You an' I, Dinah, hab sich 'sperience good many times in de ole cabin, when de good Lor' fill our ole hearts chuck full ob de glory, den crams our mouf full ob his praises, so dat we can't pray kase we praise de Lor', and dar is no room in our heart for de debbil or sin. Berry well. Den after massa Adam get up from his knees, he blow de horn agin, an' say, 'Let de whole congregation sing,' an' dar warn't so much as a fiddle or a jewsharp in de place, but, as massa Wesley say, dey all sing lustily, all de congregation, an' purty soon de soun' went way up to hebben, an' de Lor' he like de singing so well dat he come down to heah it; den de angels come down an' set on de limb ob de tree an' sing too. Den all de sons ob God heah de singin' up on de odder plantation, an' dey 'gan to shout for joy; den all de stars jine in an' sing too, an' dat's de way massa Jack say de Methodists use to sing 'fore dey got de fiddle in de gallery, an' de Lor' would allers come down an' heah dem, an' all de people for many mile aroun' would come an' heah de Methodists sing. Berry well.

Massa Adam went on dis way a good many yeahs, an' de Lor' use to come down ebbery little while an' make a wisit, see how he git along, an' ax him if he want anyting. Bye and bye Adam got mos' hunderd yeahs ole; mos' an ole bachelor in dese times, but twan't noting in dose days. Berry well. De Lor' come an' see Adam agin, an' fine he look sorry. Den de Lor' say:

"What de matter, Adam? what is you sorry about? Don't ebbryting go right on de plantation?"

Den Adam say, "'Spect so."

Den de Lor say, "What de matter, Adam?"

Den Adam say he can't keep de Lor's command-ment if he try eber so hard. Dat is what make he sorry. Den de Lor say,

"What commandment?'

Den massa Adam straighten up an look de Lor in de eye, an ax de Lor if he didn't command he, dat time when he so happy, to multiply, be fruitful and 'plenish de earth, an hab whole bunch little Adams; an now, O Lor, how I'se gwine to 'bey dis command-ment under dese yer circumstance?"

Massa Adam stick to de Lor, an tell him he done

better by de beasts an fowls, kase he did not ax dem to do anyting dey could not 'form."

Den de Lor say to massa Adam,

"Didn't I gib yer great office, make yer king ob all de animals an birds, an all dat ar kine ob glory?"

Den Adam say he hab nuff dat ar kine ob glory; he would gib de whole ob it, an more too, if de Lor will gib he a wife.

Now, Dinah, de Lor know all de time dat it wasn't good for Adam to be alone. He make him sorry, so he gin to feel de want ob a wife, make he beg hard for her, kase den he know how to 'preciate a wife. He lub her four times more. Dinah," said the preacher, giving her a gentle jog, with a kind of playful wink, "you an I had some 'sperience in dese tings."

"Dat s so," said Dinah, "I 'member dem tings berry well. Good many 'sperience such tings to-day in de worl. Dat's what make dem feel sorry, like massa Adam, kase dey not married."

"Berry well. De nex ting de Lor do he gib massa Adam some ob de chloform (chloroform); pretty soon he lie down under de palm tree an go inter deep sleep. Den de Lor take out he sharp knife, cut open massa Adam's side, an take out one ob he ribs and lay it on de table. Den close up he side and make he well, an dat Dinah, war de fust drop ob pure blood dat war shed on de earth, an dis war to make a wife for de fust

Adam. Jes four tousan (thousand) yar from dat ar, war de nex pure blood from de bleedin side ob de second Adam to purify for hissef a royal partner, de Lamb's wife. Berry well. Now de Lor he gin to make missa Adam. De fust ting he do, he cut up dat crooked bone inter tree hunder an tirty four pieces. Some for de legs, some for de arms, some for de teef, and ebryting else for de building. Den de Lor didn't stop till he finis de job, an dat's de way he allers do wid ebrybody, if we is as willin to let he do as missa Adam was. Berry well. Den de Lor breeve de life inter her, an she gan to open her bright eyes, an de rose an de lily gan to glow on her cheek, and de Lor say:

"Fus rate; good deal more handsomer dan Adam."

By dis time massa Adam he wake up to what goin on; den de Lor introduce her to Adam an he say:

"Adam, dis young missa Ebe."

Den de Lor go off a little way inter de garden, jus' as de ole folks sometimes go to bed so de young folks make de bargain. You an I, Dinah," said Sam, "hab some 'sperience in dat ar business."

"Dat's so," said Dinah.

"Berry well. Den de Lor he come back an fine de bargain all made, kase dey had no ole lubers to git rid ob. Dey had berry short courtship. You know de

Bible say, when Jacob fus saw Rachel dat he fall in lub wid her an kiss her."

"An he cry, I 'spect, for joy," said Aunt Dinah.

"Den," said Sam, "he stick to her fourteen years till he marry her. Jacob said de time didn't seem long kase he lub her all de time, but twan't so wid massa Adam an Ebe. De Lor he come back an make short work. Den he took Ebe's han in massa Adam's han, an said:

"Hole tight."

Den de Lor fus tell bofe ob dem dey mus lub one anoder all dey know how."

"An," interrupted Dinah, "dat's de kine ob wax dat stuck you an I togeder so long, Sam."

"Berry well," said Sam. "De nex ting de Lor say to massa Adam, he mus be good to her and comfort her; an he say to Ebe, you mus serve him, be a good wife, an keep house an childern clean. Den de Lor called der names Adam, and dat's de reason why de woman lose der name an is called after der husban.

"One ting more," said de Lor, "an I is done."

Den he say to Ebe dat her desire shall be to her husban, an he shall rule over her."

At this point Sam began to be a little quizzical, and, giving Dinah a nudge, said:

"Mark dat, Dinah, dat de husban shall rule ober de

wife, an dat de wife shall obey him. Dat is, de Lor tell who shall wear de breeches."

Dinah was a little jostled at this, and rose upon her feet.

"Young missus say," said she, "dat de preacher don't hab noting to say now-a-days bout dis ere 'bedience, when he marry young folks, kase de gals don't like it berry well."

So Dinah, as she supposed she had convinced Uncle Sam that this portion of the marriage covenant had become obsolete, again resumed her sitting. The rain still pouring down in copious torrents, Uncle Sam resumed his theological discourse.

"Arter dis," said he, "dey lib togedder in dere honeymoonism a good many years like Abraham an' Sarah, an' dere was no little Isaac to 'scape from de wooden bowl, running 'bout de parlor floor, an' like a little rogue paddling inter all mischief. You understand what I means by dat ar, Dinah?"

To this his auditory gave a significant bow, as much, as like the Dutchman, to say, "I fushta." Light by this time began to flash into Dinah's mind as to what the forbidden fruit might be, and she began to hitch about in her seat a little, and gave the preacher a gentle nudge, as much as to say, hurry on.

"You know," said Uncle Sam, "I hab ofen tole you an' de chillen de story 'bout de little mouse under de wooden bowl; how dat Sally's master gib her all de keys, so she could go all ober de house, an' enter ebry closet, but dat she mus' not lif up de wooden bowl on the parlor floor, no how. Jes so de Lor' say to massa Adam and Ebe; dey might hab all de fruit dey want 'cept one, an' dat was de tree ob knowledge ob good an' ebil, or 'sperience tree.

"Let me 'splain what de word knowledge mean. You know when Joseph had libed wid de virgin Mary for a good while he got offended an' was gwine to sen' her off, kase he said he had never *known* her; dat mean 'sperience. An' you know too, Dinah, dat when Cain go to de "lan' ob Nod," he see his wife and he *know* her; dat is, he hab 'sperience 'bout dis tree ob knowledge, an' in a little while dere was a leetle mouse on de carpet, which dey call Enoch."

"Oh," said Dinah, "I 'gin to see berry well."

"Well, arter a wile de Lor' come an' mak' Adam an' Ebe mornin' call. He knock, an' knock, an' fine nobody home. Den he 'gin to call, "Adam! Adam!" No answer. By an' by de Lor' hear little Cain cryin' 'hind de current bushes, an' den de Lor' know all 'bout it. Den massa Adam 'gin to lay it on missa Ebe, an' missa Ebe lay it on de ole serpent.

"Now, Dinah, dare is one ting I forget to tole you, dat dey was all dis time naked, an' de Bible say dat dey war not 'shamed. Dey war jes like naked leetle gals an' boys tree four year ole, in de nursery, in dar native innocency; dey aint 'shamed for noting, kase dey dont know noting, no how."

By this time the case was as clear in Dinah's mind as a sunbeam.

"Den," said Sam, "de Lor' ax dem what dey got on de apron for."

At this revelation, another sky rocket of light exploded in Dinah's intellect; and she jumped up and slapped her hands, and looking the preacher full in the eye, exclaimed:

"Dar, dont let me har ole feller any more from yer, dat de Odd Fellows an' de Masons havn't got de Bible on dar side. I har de preacher an' ole massa say dat dey is a hebenly institution; and dar is whar de Odd Fellows an' Masons aprons is from, kase dey wars dem in de same place as massa Adam an' Ebe war dem, an' clar it is, ole Sam, jes as clar as Ham's blanket; an' massa Dabis (Davis) secession is all in de Bible, an' Ise gwine to stick to dat."

Before the preacher had time to rally from Dinah's knock down Bible argument, the rain ceased, the driver's whip began to crack, and the preacher and his audience again seized their hoe handles.

But I am now personally interested, for I see that a silver-gray customer has entered the store of my new master, and I always feel, on such occasions, much as the negroes do when they see a trader in flesh and blood stalking about the plantation, as more or less of them expect to be sold. But this customer, as I very soon learned, was a blind man, led by a black eyed son of his, about nine or ten years old, whom he called Maxwell. After the usual morning salutations, relating to the health of his body, the merchant was then enquired of in relation to the state of his soul. This query was answered chiefly by hawks and hems, my master being seized about that time with a sudden cold. The blind customer then enquired for a piece of shirting, when my master laid his hands on me, drew me from the shelf, and gracefully laid me upon the counter, this doing perfectly oblivious of his cold, and without the least hawking or hemming. His voice was now as melodious as a German flute, his tongue played as glibly as if it had been newly oiled; and if I had to be, like Enoch, translated to heaven, the character which my master gave me would have been a sufficient passport through the pearly gates. I was now sold, in consequence of the infirmities of the customer, at "about cost," and borne off in triumph as a willing captive by my new and fifth master, whom, with your permission, dear reader, I will introduce in my next chapter.

MY FIFTH MASTER.

CHAPTER FIFTEENTH.

Well, here we are, as snug as a bug in a rug, in our new home, expecting every moment that our new mistress will unfold our gentle petals, as does the gentle shower the rose-bud, and tear me all to pieces. But my maker, in his great mercy, having made me without nerves, I therefore never get excited on such occasions.

I see by the movements and measurements that my mistress intends to make me up into shirts for her husband, who has now become my master. I had so conspicuous a place upon the shelves for a tell-tale, that I am now to be honored with a still more desirable place for my business, as I shall not only walk with him, but also sleep with him, and thus become familiar with his acts and works, and the cogitations of his reflective mind in his night visions.

By the by, reader, if you have read the introduction of this book, you have had a bird's eye peep at my present lord and master, and learned that his occupation upon week days is author, publisher and binder of books, and on the Sabbath he is a kind of poor house and prison preacher; the one with whom I contracted to publish my "Tell-Tale" and bring into light many of the sayings and doings of my twelve masters. He has already sent forth into the world nearly forty thousand volumes of his own various publications.—Among the first was the history of his own life, entitled, "Trials and Triumphs, or the Life of G. W. Henry; or Travels in Egypt;" "Twilight and Beulah;" so that with the particulars of the acts and sayings of my present master, my reader may be already familiar. Therefore, I shall be expected to say but little in the short chapter I have to write. Suffice it to say, he was a wild youth. With him, business, dancing and attendance upon ladies made up the staple of his early life, and so I have not time to speak in particular of his coal burning, blacksmithing, bell making, pocket-book manufacturing, and village building until 1827, when he commenced his career on the public works.

Perhaps no individual now living in the United States can travel over more miles of canals and railroads of his own constructing in the States of Pennsylvania, Maryland and Virginia than my present master, until he was taken blind in 1842, while furnishing timber for forty miles of railroad, stretching westward from Harper's Ferry, in Virginia, along the southern banks of the Potomac. The last portion of this earth he ever gazed upon, except in mental conception, was nineteen years ago, when he stood upon the ground where John Brown sanctified the halter and scaffold as an altar to freedom.

I have a good notion, reader, to tarry a moment in our excursion trip and give you an outline description of the first railroad celebration in any State in the Union, which was held in the birth place of this child of providence, who though but thirty years old, has grown to such monstrous proportions as to extend its limbs and iron nerves nearly all over our little creation.

It was in about 1830, I think, that my master was tearing down stupendous mountain peaks, and tumbling them into the deep ravines on the eastern slope of the Allegany Mountains, preparatory to the footfalls of the iron horse. Having finished four miles, commencing at Hollydaysburg, Pa., and running westward to the foot of the first inclined plane, it was proposed to celebrate the Fourth of July, by having a Railroad Excursion.

My master had at that time but two railway cars, with four small wheels to each. On these were mounted something like large hay racks, or rather they resembled two storied hen coops, and as there was not at that time a locomotive in the United States, four large Pennsylvania horses were hitched before them, as a motive power. As the news spread, the entire novelty of the occasion, drew the people in, as with a net, from glen and mountain, valley and plain for many miles around. Men and boys were there, cripples and crazy, old and young, from the babe to the venerable grandmother. Altogether they were the most free and easy multitude that ever assembled.

Those who had shoes wore them; those who had none went without. Tangled-headed beaux, and bear-headed bells, who had never heard of a corset, or of crinoline were there, and thickly studded the excited multitude, never heeding the trampled toes, or the jostlings of the lookers on in Venice.

As we were about to move off with the train, the cripples, grandmothers and babies were about all that could be crowded into the cars. The driver now cracked his whip, the train began to move slowly on, being aided in its onward march by the strong shoulders of the enthusiastic crowd, which, like spears of grass thronged the line of procession, and thus matters went on until the four miles were passed over in considerable more than four minutes of time. Now the frugal banquet was spread, and toasts without number, hit or miss, were freely uttered.

My master being one of the "Lions of the day," was toasted brown; among the toasts, as I afterwards discovered on an old slip of newspaper, was the following, given by old Senator Garber. He being filled with the spirit, spoke of my master as making the first piece of railroad, and as making the first railroad car in the United States, as well as inaugurating the first railroad celebration. He wound up thus: "Captain Henry, may he go to heaven on a railroad."

All this narration, reader I will acknowledge, is "switching off" from the drift and design of this work. The story of the first expedition of Christopher Columbus; Fulton's first steamboat paddled up the Hudson; or the railroad celebration, the account of which you have just read, will excite little or no interest; but if you, Ripvanwinkle like, had fallen asleep at the birth of these three children of Providence, and awaked you in 1860, when they shed their milk-teeth; you would wonder what their growth and perfection might be thirty years hence.

I believe it will generally be conceded by those who have read the narration of my master, concerning himself, that he has given a fair portrait of the whole man, without concealing the warts, scars and other imperfections. But Tell Tale Rag has a secret to reveal, that the readers of my master's life are strangers to, and oh how I am distressed until I tell it. Twice when my master was writing his life, and revising it, he came to this snubbing post. But the picture looked so mean to him, and the memory thereof was so abhorrent, that his old goose quill refused to wag or shed a black tear on the manuscript in memento of its foibles.

But as I have roasted my other masters without mixture of mercy, my present one shall not escape the disclosures of "Tell Tale Rag;" even though he kicks the manuscript out of doors, and refuses to publish the book for me.

About the time of which I am now writing, my master might be said to be in the zenith of his worldly glory. He was the owner of a fine farm, lying at the base of the Allegany Mountains, on which he had erected mills, stores, dwelling houses and shops. This young city was called "Henrysburg," and of it he was Post Master, under the reign of Amos Kendall, who was at that time Postmaster General. In addition to this place a batallion of laborers, with numerous teams "hawed and gee'd" at his beck.

"Let him that thinketh he standeth, take heed lest he fall."

If the mechanic commences his tower at its base and rises gradually with each layer of brick or stone, he can rise to the skies without becoming dizzy. But if he takes a sudden flight from the bottom to the cap stone, his brain will reel as he sweeps his eye around on new and dazzling wonders. And if he falls, alas! to what depths of degradation is he driven. Sudden, and what are called high-flights in religion, have a different tendency: as the spirit becomes deformed by its nearer view of heaven, it becomes humbled. But in this "he that is low need fear no fall."

What monarch is this we now behold strutting and swelling like a peacock in his palace? Who is casting his eyes around, and in soliloquy, saying: "Is not this great Babylon, which I have builded?" Is this not my honor and glory? Look again: We see the same man in fetters of brass, grazing in the fields like an ox. His hair is matted like the eagle's feathers, and his nails are like the talons of a foul bird; and thus he continued until he had learned duty in the school of God, "who casteth down the scornful and knoweth the proud afar off." The son of this same monarch twelve years after, when standing on the platform of his glory, surrounded by a thousand guests, about to drink his health in the golden goblets brought from the Temple in Jerusalem; and to toast him with, "Oh King, live forever!" saw the hand-writing upon the walls; Cyrus was at the gate, and one hour swept Prince and people into eternity.

But, says the reader, enough of that. Give us the secret if you have any.

Well, to resume, then. About this time President Andrew Jackson had removed the deposites from the

Bank of the United States, and old Nick Biddle, in order to wreak *his* vengeance, locked all the treasury vaults in the Keystone State. My master now began to reel and tumble. Although he *finished* his contract under the most rigid embarassments, yet poverty, like Cyrus at the gates, laid him flat upon his back. Ichabod was written on every thing that he, a few months previously, had called his own, and his earthly glory departed.

My master now, in order to recover that which was lost, engaged in the same business as did the prodigal son, when *his* earthly glory departed. He went to feeding swine with slops from the Devil's distillery. My master was a stranger to retreat. He soon gained his feet, and in a short time he reared and became the master of a large hotel, and breakfasted the passengers on the railcars. The front of this building, supported by huge columns, looked over handsome graveled walks and green plots, from whence arose rare shade trees. In the rear was a beautifully arranged garden, on the background of which was a green turf, shaded with fruit trees, whose very leaves blushed at the ridiculous scenes which they o'ershadowed. Here my master had erected what was called a "shuffle board," adapted to an Irish game. At a little distance was a ten-pin alley.

I see as I write that my master's face is flushed al-

[8]

ternately with the scarlet of indignation and the crimson of shame, seemingly about to kick himself out of the door; but he must grin and bear it, for I am not half through.

Still back of the garden, there was a fence gate opening into another grass plot, and was bordered by a mill dam. On this ground my master erected a gallows, I should think thirty or forty feet high, on which he used to hang his customers. Do not be frightened yet, timid reader, as they were not cruelly hanged by their necks, but seated on a sort of palanquin. There my master would pull off his coat and swing this long pendulum to a giddy height, and woe to the man who was so drunk or woman who was so dizzy as to fall out. But I see that your head swims, and so we will go back into the hotel.

The bar-room was hung about with some ridiculous caricatures, or prints of the times. The bar, the palisade of King Alcohol, was interlined with looking-glass reflectors, the shelves were literally burdened with cut glass decanters filled with venomous serpents, tumblers, &c., &c. The usage of this bar and grounds was, that for every game played, &c., there were to be so many drinks paid for at the bar. In the upper story was a ball room.

But I see that my master is getting sick at his stomach at the remembrance of the past, and would fain be bathed in the Lethe of forgetfulness. If there is any mudsill in hell lower than that upon which the rumseller stands, pouring out three cents worth of liquid damnation for the poor, miserable inebriate, somebody's father or brother, I am ignorant of it. Yes, there is one peg lower still. If it is wicked to girdle the old trees so that they wither and die, how much more so the young and thrifty nursery, the hope of the church and the world? Even so the man in his first-class hotel, who presses to the lips of my son the first ruinous glass, should receive the greater damnation. All this was done by my master, backed up and sanctioned by the law of the land, and his license recommended by church members and moralists. Now, reader, can you wonder at or blame my master for skipping over this foul blot on his character? How glad I am he has found a place for repentance in the day of salvation.

This, thirty years ago, was one of the fashionable sins of the day, but I am thankful that religion, morality and common decency does, in this day, despise and abhor, as does now my master, any legislature or commissioner who will grant a license to any rumseller to murder the innocent and lay them in premature graves. But alas! there are sins, fashionable sins, tolerated and bowed to both in church and State, if possible as damning and deceptive as rum, but they are concealed under the apron of fig leaves; they are the chloroform of a false peace. Some of them, by the help of the Lord, I will drag from their hiding places before I close this volume.

CHAPTER SIXTEENTH.

Once more, my friend, if you have your trunk checked and ticket purchased, we will get on the excursion train and take notes by the way. We will turn, with disgust, our backs upon this symmetrical spider web of King Alcohol, and thank God for our deliverance, for in his mercy and wrath he has cursed this traffic, and ever blights the hopes and fortunes of at least nine-tenths of its votaries, as was the experience of my present master. He left this sink of sin in about the same condition as the prodigal son when he turned his back to his swine feeding.

But I see we must hop, skip and jump over a thousand and one things in the history of my present master. Now we see him engaged on about thirty miles of the Cumberland Valley and Franklin railroad; now on the "Tide Water" canal; from thence to the Lancaster railroad; now we find him scooping out the Chesapeake and Ohio canal; and finally we leave him with a steam saw mill in the glens of the Virginia mountains. Now, reader, we have come to another

Pike's Peak in his history. The wings of his worldly glory have perched his ambitious mind on one of the highest twigs of the loftiest cedar. Now place yourself in a position where you can see him tumble down with both wings and legs broken by the fowler.

The place where he had erected his steam saw mill was in the midst of a forest of stately oaks and lofty pines. There was not a school-house nor church on the Virginia side within eleven miles; nothing but dreary mountains and ravines, with here and there an old house said to be deserted in consequence of being haunted by spooks, hobgoblins, &c. I now behold my master seated on a log by the side of his friend, General C. It was on Saturday night in the month of August, 1841.

"Now," said he to the General, giving him at the same time a slap on the shoulder, "I have had any amount of bad luck in my life, but I can now feel an independent fortune on the ends of my fingers, and that, too, within the short space of six months. I have, at this time, from twenty to twenty-five mills in my employ, shipping from Havre de Grace, Washington City, and other places that which will soon lay about two million feet of timber upon my contract.—My new steam mill which I have just finished you see works to a charm, and to-morrow," said he, "being the Sabbath, we will go to Berkley Springs, (which was a watering place about eleven miles distant,) dine, take a julep or two with the planters, cut a swell, jump Jim Crow and return."

Alas! reader, how little we know what a day will bring forth.

The Sabbath morning came, the golden king of day like its maker poured forth its beams upon the evil and the good; on the Sabbath breaker and the Sabbath keeper; on the tares and the wheat. My master's family then consisted of his wife, little Fanny, who was about two and a half years; and her little infant sister, Florence. Let me say here, for rag as I am, I do think that the dove would become weary in searching for a fairer piece of porcelain than Fanny. Now reader, if you are not an old bachelor, you will not be offended if we tarry a while and gaze upon this blooming Ceres. Her mind was in advance of her age, she had a model face, exquisite form, and well cut mouth. The rose and lily played together upon her face, diving sometimes down into the dimples, then rising, and perching, and spreading their wings o'er her plump cheek. Her black sparkling eyes would subdue and captivate a battalion of young Zouaves; at all events, she had her father well bound with the silken cords of love.

Breakfast being over, my master and family, together with General C——, mounted the carriage, cracked the whip, and under full sail moved towards the halls of banqueting, mirth and Sabbath breaking, but when my master had gone about two miles on his journey, in the dark glen of the mountain, a Lion leaped into the road, as much as to say, "thus far shalt thou go, and no farther," and here thy ambitious ways shall be stayed. I afterwards learned that it was the same Lion that crossed the track of Saul of Tarsus, on his way to Damascus, known as the Lion of the tribe of Judah. Let me here say, that a few rods previous to his halting, my master from a state of perfect health, was taken with an indescribable trembling, a sort of nondescript feeling coming all over him. The carriage was now wheeled about and returned to the Mills. While my master was lying in a suffering state upon the bed, little Fanny went out into the woods and gathered a boquet of flowers, to comfort and cheer her idolizing father. I now in mental vision see her coming in, clad in a rich straw colored shally, with white satin stripes, which her father had purchased previous to her birth. But that was the first and last day she ever wore it; for after cheerfully eating her supper with the family, as usual, she sat down in her little chair and reclined her head forwards, as her mother supposed, to go to sleep. At that moment a large wolf entered the door, and opening his ravenous jaws, closed them upon her, and held her thus about fifteen minutes, quivering in his jaws.

When my master was a child his heart was set upon the possession of a yellow bird which had made a nest on the premises of his grandfather. One day one flew into the house and was secured for him, a string about ten or fifteen feet long was tied to its legs so it could fly, but not get away.

With a heart overflowing with joy, he went with his bird to the house where his mother resided; but on the way the old cat sprang from her lair, and seizing the bird between her teeth began to pull in one way, while he pulled in another. His grief was terrible.

It was somewhat so when in the time to which allusion has been made, the wolf seized little Fanny. My master was then without the joys of religion, but was beginning to tumble down where it might be obtained. As it was with his bird experience, so now his heart was filled with commingled sorrow and murmuring. From that time all Virginia was to him as a grave yard. Crape seemed to hang upon all the boughs of the trees, and grief was stalking on his every pathway.

But here let us learn a lesson of human nature from the doings of my master. The rum selling affair was surely wicked enough to be ashamed of; but I shall now bring to light an inquiry still deeper dyed, and which I believe in the sight of God is equally condemned because it is more deceptive, common and fashionable. The scene of which I am about to speak, was enacted in a dark corner of my master's bedroom, on the night following the death of Fanny.

The mother having retired and sobbed herself to sleep, my master bidding the watchers of the marble form of his Fanny "good night," retired to his bed room. Before unrobing for the night, he blew out the candle, as every one does who is about to do anything they are ashamed of, and walking carefully in his stocking feet to the corner of the room, he for the first time since his boyhood bowed his stubborn knees before God.

The first thing he did, was to tell a square up and down lie to his sovereign; I see reader you start back at the very mention of such audacity in my master; but be careful that you do not do the same thing every day, for I would have you understand that lying to God is one of the most common, deceptive and fashionable sins of the day.

Well, you say reader, give us the facts in the case. I will resume, and would say, that, after a heated debate between my master's carnal heart and his lips, his tongue prevailed and made his lips tell the Lord that he wanted religion. I have often heard my master say, that if Christ had answered his request, salvation with its cross, his heart so proud and wicked would have spurned it and cast it back in disgust. Alas, how many draw nigh to God with their lips, while their heart is far from him; are glued to the world, the flesh and the Devil.

See that mother: she is telling that prattling babe as it begins to claw for the spectacles, "I'll throw you to the dogs," "I'll give you a sound whipping," and the next moment almost devour it with kisses. It was somewhat similar with my master; he hated sin about as much as the mother hated her babe.

When a man beholds himself covered with scabs and corruption, produced by the small pox, he will show his hatred to the loathsome disease, by using every means in his power for getting rid of it. And, so the true penitent, while he prays, will at the same time kick the cur of his vileness out of the door. Until hypocrites can be brought low enough to lift the coffin lids of their own hearts, and behold, the corruption and dead men's bones, their lips will continually lie to God, when they talk about hating sin, and like my master, continue to roll it upon their tongues as children do delicious sugar plums.

Well, reader, you seem to be surprised that such iniquity should be brought to light by my tell-tale tongue. But tarry a while; I am only half done with this rehearsal. Before my master was arisen from his knees, that old slaveholder, the Devil, began to be alarmed lest he should lose one more of his faithful servants, who at this time began looking at the North star. As this was a critical case, his Satanic majesty, distrusting his ambassadors, came in person to see what was to be done. He was clad in a white gauze dress, which was cast over his black suit, and as he spake in pleasant tones, appeared to be very reasonable.

"Religion," said he, "is an excellent thing, and I advise you by all means to obtain it. You know, sir, that you have set a hundred times when you would obtain the prize, which were a thousand fold more favorable than the present."

My master then gave a gentle nod of his head, and said:

"That is very true, sir."

"Now," said his Satanic majesty, "is the most inauspicious time that could be presented. You have hardly time to eat or sleep from the pressure of business. You ought to have at least six months to repent in. And then, what time have you for family prayers, and forty other things that will have to be dragged in to interfere with your business hours? I suggest, therefore," said he, "that you suspend getting religion until you get through your contracts, get your affairs settled up with the world, and then get religion."

My master that moment signed the contract, agreed to serve the Devil six months longer, and his majesty left for a season with a grin upon his face.

A very gentle dove, which I had perceived hovering round the room, was terribly grieved with this contract, dropped a tear or two, left the room, and in heaven reported this disgraceful conduct of my master. Moses said, "Cut him down," but Christ interfered, and proposed to give master another tumble down the steeps of pride and ruin. Now, right on the back of this contract, ere yet he arose from his knees, happened a little big thing that I will mention. There was a ten-penny nail that had started from the rough floor, perhaps a quarter of an inch. In rising, my master hit his knee against it; an affair which, at the time, seemed to be but trifling. He then crawled into bed, and soon fell asleep on his pillow of carnal security. Well, to make a long story short, his limb soon began to be swollen and very distressing. Important business called him to Martinsburg, Va., but not being able to return, he lay, a dreadful sufferer, six weeks at a hotel, in which time he was brought near the grave, and here was a scene of more hypocritical praying and lying to God. To illustrate his position, suffer me to relate an affair that was told me by a rag which was a bed-fellow in the scavenger's rag-bag.

He said his master had a sore quarrel with a neighboring farmer, which was of long standing. They hated each other so intensely that they would not unite their line fences, so each built a fence near the line, making what is commonly called "the devil's lane."

"It came to pass," said he, "that sickness brought my master nigh death's door, and he began to think it advisable to make friends with his neighbor before he crossed the swellings of Jordan. They soon had an interview in the sick chamber, and in short agreed to be friends, destroy the devil's lane, and unite their fence as good neighbors should. They then shook hands, and the neighbor started for the door to take his departure. At this moment my master suddenly aroused.

"Hold a moment, John," said he, "if I die this time, let it be understood that the fence is to come down; but if the good Lord thinks proper to raise me up again, the lane is to be kept up."

This was about the substance, as the Lord understood my master's prayers: if he died, he wanted salvation, but if he got well, as the sequel will show, he did not wish to be bothered with it.

And now, reader, we come to another deception, and a prevalent sin of the day. If my master or the fence man had been stretched out in death, they would most assuredly have been preached to heaven.

"How penitent he was!" would the ministers have said, "And how fervently he prayed," would say all the friends.

Alas! what whitewashing is performed on dying

beds, what false hopes are buried in the grave, and what heavenly eulogies are inscribed on the marble erected by false friendship to their memory!

CHAPTER SEVENTEENTH.

Reader, if I had an apothecary's mortar that would hold the Atlantic, and should place in it all the iniquities spoken of in the Bible as pertaining to man, and then should gather in all the named and nameless ones among the fallen sons of Adam, and compound them together into one pill, yet there is a single sin, as common as household furniture, and so popular and fashionable that it is entertained in almost every family yea, courted and petted in almost every caste of society — that would outweigh all the other sins in the mortar, and of this sin my master was basely guilty. You have, dear reader, but a faint view of the magnitude of his sinfulness at the time of which I am writing. This sin was INGRATITUDE TO GOD!

Alas! how many fond parents' hearts have been bruised and mangled by this polished sledge hammer, as stroke after stroke has been laid on by that ungrateful son or daughter for whom they have worn out their lives; whom they have fed, clothed and educated.—"Had it been an enemy," said David, "I could have borne it." No one can drive a lancet so deep, or leave a wound so hard to heal, as "the familiar friend," when deceived and enslaved by this common, unthought of sin of ingratitude.

There are some, however, that would render all homage and obedience to parents and the world generally, who would rob God at the same time of the honors due unto Him as their king; and Jesus Christ of their services which he has purchased with his own blood; and their own souls of salvation and the joys of heaven, and still imagine themselves honest and highly respectable.

Oh, that such men and women could, spiritually, be turned inside out, that they might discover in the sunlight of truth that they are a traveling synagogue of Satan; while at the same time some of them are gracing, or rather disgracing, like the rotten-hearted Pharisees, the highest seats in the synagogue. I once heard an infidel remark of such, that they would steal the Lord's supper and pocket the table cloth.

Allow me, just at this point, to relate a fact to which I was personally knowing, which happened in Pennsylvania in the year 1830.

The rulers of a very popular church made a redundant preparation of "shew bread" and wine for the Lord's Supper, and after the congregation was dispersed, these rulers would tarry about the altar and eat up the fragments of bread and drain the jug of the last drop of the consecrated wine, and so leave the sanctuary filled with the spirit. If it had been the kind taken from Bozra, it would have blown every one of these old leathern Pharisaical bottles to atoms, and there would have been nothing left of them.

But it is time to hunt up my master. He is up and dressed by this time, and ready for another direction, or post mortem examination, as the case may be. This is scorching business, I know; but a "sanctified recklessness" is careful for nothing but how we may best please God and destroy the works of the Devil. We left my master reduced to a skeleton at the Martinsburg hotel, but we hail him this morning at his Kinderhook steam mills, swinging his emaciated leg on a pair of wooden crutches. As Bunyan would say, he had again seized hold of the muck rake, and began to rake together the remains of a scattered fortune, or rather digging a grave to bury out of sight his solemn covenant promises made to Christ on his bed of languishing while lying at the hotel, when plank after plank was being swept from under his feet.

Heralds now came, as in the days of Job, treading upon each others' heels, into his chamber of sickness, telling him of the partial failure of the railroad company; another of the depreciation of the currency; the third of a broken engine; while the fourth, to cap the climax, told of the unusual drought, drying up every fountain of water, and clogging every wheel of his many mills.

The dove again with tearful eye and weary wing reported in heaven the stubborn rebellion of my wicked master, how he had despised the riches of grace and forbearance of God. Moses at once drew out his newly whetted sword, but mercy, at that moment discovering several bottles of tears, which like dew drops had been gathered for about thirty years from the cheeks of a pious mother who had shed them over her only son and child, seized the naked blade with her hands, and persuaded Moses to sheath again his sword until one more tumble down of his ambition could be effected. This was agreed upon in the councils of heaven, to be his last trial, and that if my master did not ground the weapons of his rebellion he should then be cut down as a cumberer of the ground.

The wheels of his mills by this time had begun slowly to move, his flesh had resumed its usual plumpness, and health sat upon his brow. All was right and natural except the knee which had been injured by the tenpenny nail, on the night when the awful covenant was made with heaven and hell. This limb, like Jacob's when he wrestled with the angel, was shrunken and withered, from the hollow of his thigh to his ankle, and swung around like a dead branch; as my master moved around upon his crutches. But in about a year after his conversion it resumed its former size and strength. Now reader, we come to the last, and yet most glorious tumble to the foot of the tree, where lay the axe of repentance.

My master's sight, without a particle of pain or inflamation, began to leave him; just about as gradually as daylight would be submerged into midnight darkness on a summer's night.

My master, I discover as I write, is getting downright happy. This spot of his experience has always been to him a sacred one. I once heard a very pious and eminent minister of the gospel relate the scenes which tinged with gold the clouds of his repenting hours. He said, one providence after another brought him to the root of a large beech tree in the dense forest one dark and dismal night, where he kneeled down on a soft bed of moss, where he made a solemn vow to the Prince of grace, that he would never rise from his knees until his sins were all forgiven, and his name registered in heaven. Bitter scalding tears swelled the banks of his guilty cheeks, and moistened the thick moss on which he kneeled, and a little before the break of day a carrier pigeon brought in his beak salvation. His tears increased, but they were then as sweet as the dew-drops from the rose of Sharon, as they still showered the moss; and, he said, as he arose from his knees with a shout of triumph, he gathered up a handful of the saturated moss, and carried it home and showed it to his friends, which he still preserved as a precious relic; and when he was buried, he should order it placed in his cold hands. And if, with his body, all should be reduced to ashes, he would even gather up the ashes of the moss and, in the resurrection morning, take it in his hands to Jesus, telling him that on that moss he was made an heir of heaven. So, also, this spot was equally sacred to my master. I have often heard him compare himself at this point to an old canal horse after he had been worn out on the tow-path: totally blind, half skinned by the galling harness, starved to a skeleton, not worth knocking down, but turned out by the cruel driver to graze a few days in the corners of the fence, and then keel over and die.

This was the glorious position in which the world and Christ found him in 1842. One tumble more would have sent him beyond the reach of mercy.

Notwithstanding this terrible portrait we have faintly drawn of my then wicked master, he was numbered among the honorable and respectable in the society of the world. He was called a gentleman, entertained and visited in the first circles of society, and called a good-hearted and clever fellow. This is weighing a man, a sinner, in the false, deceptive and fashionable balances of this world; at the same time, if he had been weighed in the balances of the sanctuary of the God of David, he would have been found wanting. Yes, wanting everything to recommend him to the courts of heaven, but, like the withered branch of the vine, only prepared for the rake and the flames.

The six months' league, or contract, with his Satanic majesty was about concluded, and now he began to look for the star in the east instead of the star of the north. His Egypt to him with all his glory was blasted, and he began to start with good earnest for the promised land. But it turned out as the Devil told him: it took him six months to do up his repentance before he could cross the red sea and shout with the exulting multitude, "The horse and his rider are overthrown."

But we should consume all the space in this book if we should undertake to describe all the meanderings and slimy snail tracks of my master in this awful yet glorious six months. It is impossible for the physician, with all his panaceas and poultices, while there is proud flesh in the wound, to heal it. Nothing but the burning caustic will sear it down so that it can be mollified and healed; and it took the great physician of souls about six months, with the searing caustic of conviction, daily and hourly applied, to burn out the proud flesh and destroy the worldly wisdom of his impatient patient. None but the tallest preachers and mighty cedars of Lebanon were capable of addressing such a dignitary as he, until finally he found a receipt in an old book, whose author's name was Paul, which read as follows:

"Let no man deceive himself. If any man seem to be wise in this world, let him become a fool that he may be wise."

My master swallowed this receipt, and it sent out the disease from within like measles or small-pox, so that he began to abhor himself in dust and ashes, and, like Naaman, began to dive to the bottom of old Jordan, and the seventh time, his filthiness and leprosy went overboard, and with one mighty bound he leaped into the kingdom of grace and shouted glory.

And now, reader, suffer us to show you another destructive and fashionable sin. I mean poulticing *convicts* with untempered mortar and then calling them *converts*. To illustrate what I mean, I must deal in parables:

There was a little boy once came to the nest of an old hen, which was about hatching her brood. Some of the little prisoners had got fairly out of jail. The little fellow, in order to assist nature and at once let every prisoner free, prematurely broke their shells.—The chickens gave one faint peep as they came out, a gape and a stretch, and that was the last that was heard from them.

Alas! how many thousands have listened to the declaration of peace from some "fusion minister" or member, before God had spoken peace. The devil tried this on my master several times, but he indignantly threw the deceitful poultice back in his face, and, like Rachel, refused to be comforted by a worm of the dust like himself.

Alas! how many there are that are called converts, who, like Topsy, know not that they ever were born, but "spect they growed," or are like the chickens with the shell prematurely broken by an outsider, instead of the swellings of conviction in the breast of the prisoner himself; and if you get a peep out of them in a week after, they have to be pressed like a sponge. Oh! the wickedness and damning iniquity that is concealed by this popular and fashionable white-washing.

There was a time in Egypt when there was a dead child in every house, except Goshen; and tell me a house within a hundred miles of the place in which I am now writing, that does not entertain a back slider, and perhaps a whole family, if they tell the truth, once professing religion.

And now, reader, we will look on another page of my master's life, during the six months he stood trembling in the prisoner's box, and show you what a fool the devil made of this epitome of worldly wisdom, which like pusley or Canada thistles grew so rank in the wilderness of his soul.

When Satan gave up the recovery of his fugitives, he placed another kind of bait or false fly on the hook which my master played around, and nibbled at for a long time, and had not Abraham with his seventy Zouaves come to his relief and delivered him as he did Lot, I do believe the old angler would have got the hook in his jaws, and had him pickled down in the barrel of self-righteousness, preserved unto the judgment.

Now reader, put your finger on this line so as to not lose your place, and make a visit with me to the rag family in the scavenger's bag; as Uncle Sam says,—"we'll have little 'sperience" by the way of illustration, in the exposition of this popular sin of the day. In fact, we do not wish to feed you any faster than you can clearly understand or digest, lest you get the dyspepsia. Well, here we are with a jovial set of tell-tales; our business being made known, there was a piece of sacking broke the silence, which we found in learning his history, was the left part of pious old Teddy's small clothes; he said his master had felt the arrows of conviction rankling in his soul for some time, which had been driven to the feather from the gospel bow, until at last he cried out in agony, "What shall I do to be saved." The Rev. Mr. Simon Magus then began to prescribe to the best of his knowledge, telling Teddy that he must work out his own salvation; forgetting to mix with the powder any of the healing balm, namely, that God would work in him to will and do of his pleasure. He said, Teddy, his colored master, then began to work out his salvation about as a dog would work in digging out a wood-chuck from his burrow. His hoe handle was moistened with tears during the day; and his peck of corn, which was his weekly ration, was also moistened with the bitter, scalding drops, that chased each other in hot pursuit down his ebony cheeks. He prayed, he wrestled, and he trembled; he wrung his hands in prayer until many a midnight hour; until despair began to mark him with the broad grin of a demoniac, but just in this hour of peril, at midnight, he leaped from his couch and made for his master's stable, and bowed himself at the manger, emaciated and trembling; he cried out, "oh Lordy Massa Jesus, here be poor ole black Teddy, come to de to tell all 'bout my 'fairs and troubles; Massa Magus tell me dat I mus' work de salvation wid de fear an' trembling; and now, oh Massa Jesus, ise been working night and day dese six months, and I find I gits worse and worse, and i'se don't know notin no how, and now oh Lordy Massa, if dare be any help for poor ole trembling nigga, Massa Jesus hab to do it hese'f."

That moment every chord that bound old Teddy's soul was snapped asunder, his sins rolled off into the gulf of Gehena; the old mud house, like those in Goshen, was brilliant with divine light; strength was given him and he, like Sampson of old, broke every new rope and green withe; and like that ancient Nazarite, with his unsheared locks, woven in the web, he carried off loom, yarn, beam and all, as he left the stable, shouting "glory to God on high." This was about a fac simile of my master's experience as he crossed the threshhold of the kingdom of grace.

But I see that it is time to close this already too lengthy chapter, and so we will take a lunch of Pomegranates and Figs, for we would comfort our reader with apples, and stay him with flagons by the way, and so keep him good natured, amid so many hard sayings.

CHAPTER EIGHTEENTH.

The Surgeon and Physician bring forth the dead from their silent lodgings and lay them upon the dissecting table in the rooms appropriate for that purpose by the faculty.

They then, in the presence of a class of students, take to pieces the several parts of the human frame, as the watch repairer takes in pieces the watch which is false to time, in order to discover the cause of the disease that slew the patient, and then devise both preventtives, and remedies for the benefit of the living.

Even so, we have laid our present blind master on the table for spiritual dissection, and while we were taking him to pieces, were astonished to find so great a combination of moral maladies, which were as plague spots upon his soul, eating out his life and destroying his soul.

All this we have done for the benefit of the living, hoping by the aid of the great physician, not only to make known to posterity the origin, nature and extent of the sinful disease; but also to leave for the benefit of others, some valuable recipes for their complaints, and finally, to direct them to this great physician of souls, who will furnish them a sovereign balm that will heal all manner of sicknesses and diseases, if taken in season, that human nature is heir to, without money and without price.

You will find the doors of his hospital always open, and the great physician ready, with the greatest cheerfulness to wait upon all his patients; and from the appearance, cords of crutches, wooden legs, and artificial eyes laying round the door of his office, one would suppose that many of the patients were cured or healed with the first dose, as in ancient cripple revivals, and had returned to their homes, leaping and shouting, and praising God.

We have already discovered to you, reader, three of these plague spots on the soul of my master, namely: proud flesh, worldly wisdom, and dead works, and given you a recipe for curing the same. We behold now a spot the doctors call self-conceit, mixed in a kind of a compound of self-will, being double dyed. This disease has baffled the skill of many physicians; or rather the greatest difficulty has been to get the patient to swallow the pills which are called pills of humility; they are a terrible drug to take, especially for adults. It wars almost exclusively with pride, self-conceit, &c., and it is the only pill that will lay this disease in the dust and save the patient.

Reader, you have been to the district or primary school; you saw there a tall gawky, who never saw the inside of a spelling book until he was forty years old, now trying to bend over and listen to the teachings of a little girl or boy six years old, trying to spell bag, tag, &c. This was the case with my master, he having never learned the first rudiments in the school of Christ until he was forty-two years old. It was an awful job to get his almightyness to stoop down and listen to the teachings of some little babe in Christ; one of his consequence and age would have cheerfully entered the college hall, and began if possible to study astronomy, learn to count the stars, and call each by their respective names, then laid down the cash for his tuition, and walked out, neither asking any odds of the professor or rendering any thanks. But the idea of entering in at the meek and lowly door, and that too of a free school for poor children, this was a pill that my master gagged at for months before he could get it fairly down.

David, you know, often compares the seductive devices of Satan to the fowler's snares, which are always set by the trapper, in a manner adapted to the bird of which he is in pursuit. And there is a snare in which the Virginians trap wild turkey, that range the mountains. In the first place they make a pen of rails or poles, about two feet high, and cover it over with boards; then they throw on brush carelessly as if it was a kind of accidental heap of rubbish; the lower rail is blocked up just high enough for a good sized turkey to creep under; the next and last business is to commence scattering corn from the inside of this pen to several rods distance in the roads. The design and object of the man, is a fair sample of some people's benevolence. If they give away a sixpence they expect it will return to them with a good fat turkey; but after a display of this charity the fowler goes his way just as the Devil did when he sowed tares in the wheat field; the character of a turkey, you know, reader, is what Paul would call "heady, high minded," always looking for snares, and always getting into them.—Well, we see a drove of these well dressed bipeds a coming and all at once they stumble on to this charitable institution; and being very hungry, every high head is brought to the ground and diligently searching for corn, they begin to stow away the seductive bait until they come to the lower rail of the pen, where the corn is still more profuse, until they find the whole flock crept into the pen, and when the last kernel is picked up, their leader, who on other occasions swells and struts among his flock, like a Mormon High Priest among his duplicate wives with his brandy colored face, and long black beard hanging down over his shirt bosom, now proposes a retreat.

Nicodemus was a gentleman of great wisdom and mightiness in his own conceit, and was familiar with the processes of a natural birth ; but he was as ignorant of the spiritual birth as this old Tom Turkey was, of the manner in which he was to lead his congregation out of this foul snare in which they had been taken.

All they had to do was to bow down their heads and they could with all ease have retreated and escaped under the very rail by which they had entered ; but this you know is not the nature of turkeys, or of proud sinners. Their heads were up, running to and fro in terrible dismay and confusion, bunting their heads against the boards over them.

Pictures, not unlike this, are exhibited very often in our popular and fashionable churches; more especially during times of revival, during the winter when there is nothing else to do. If all the turkeys in the spiritual mountains were gathered, with all their uncles, aunts and cousins, who have stood with them, and with tearful eyes have begged them to "stoop to conquer," to humble themselves, that they might be exalted to their native freedom; pointing them to this, as their only way of escape; telling them also that the tread of the old fowler would soon be heard, and that their high heads would cause their destruction; that they would soon be basted and roasted by him who so kindly had made their table a snare to them; all would be in vain to the majority. How many true gospel ministers have worn out their lungs in thus warning, as they stood over the open Bible; how many fathers and mothers in Israel have furrowed their cheeks with tears, begging, praying, and beseeching "heady, high-minded," ungodly sinners to bow themselves at the mourner's bench, as their only way of escape from the snare of the arch fowler. But these towering intellects, like "Trinity Steeples," grey headed in sins and iniquities, will sit or stand erect amid all these sermons, prayers and tears, as if their back bones were made of crowbars.

Presumptuous and self-willed, they will stiffen their

necks like two bulls at a fair. Plead with them to bow down at the mourner's bench, and they, like General Naaman, will get into a terrible rage, as much as to say "I'll be d—d if you get me down with those sniffling women and children, under the lower rail of the pen."

Poor fellows! when they hear the tread of the fowler, or the galloping of the pale horse and his rider over the pavements, how low will their false dignity be laid in the dust!

Alas! how deceptive, and yet how fashionable is this proud Moloch of the day.

Well, reader, I propose that we take a hop, skip and jump over many interesting events that happened to my master, until we come to the old free school house where he learned his alphabet and escaped forever from the snare of the fowler under this low rail of repentance and humility. We should be glad to tell you what a providential deliverance he had from a watery grave in Virginia, and how his proud knees refused to bend to him who delivered him from death. We could also tell you of the singular visions he had in the cities of Washington and Baltimore, and in the State of Pennsylvania. The death-like scene that took place one night at Belthoover's Hotel, in Baltimore, and how, in the same city, he was delivered at midnight from the belly of hell, under the charge of his adversary, for eating and drinking damnation to his own soul, in consequence of partaking of the holy symbols of Christ's sufferings before, as a child of God, it was his privilege, committing, as he made him believe, the unpardonable sin. But for the particulars of my master's wanderings in the desert we would refer you to his published history.

Well, here we are in the old school house, where thousands of children of the Abrahamic stock were dwelling in tents, heirs, together with Abraham, Isaac and Jacob, of the exceeding great and precious promises. There were, in one of these tents, probably about fifty men and women, a division of sexes being formed by a cloth running through the centre of the tent.—About twelve o'clock one night my master came in from a prayer meeting, where he found, as he supposed, every one in the tent fast asleep. The brethren were packed together like herring in a box, with one space left for his worn out and despairing self. He then committed his soul to God as well as he knew how, and pillowed his throbbing brow. In further illustration of his feelings up to this point, suffer me to relate a story which was told me while in the rag-bag, by one of my companions who had been used as a sticking plaster on the limbs of one of the bloated sons of Bacchus, who was often picked up by his neighbors, in the morning, from his gutter lodgings where he had spent the night.

My rag friend said, that among many experiments to restore him, his neighbors resorted to the following frightful expedient: Jake was found one very dark night, lying in the road by the side of his empty jug, sound asleep. The boys then went to the tannery and brought forth several untanned hides, stuffed them with straw, placed horns on their heads and apparently pitchforks in their hands. They then surrounded this beastly dreamer, raised a flame with straw, which made the darkness more visible, and the images to appear like horrible fiends and tormentors. Jake was then aroused from his slumbers, and, opening his eyes, horror-stricken he looked around him, beholding as he supposed, his tormentors. He now exclaimed:

"Well, here I am, waked up in hell. Just as I expected; not the least disappointed."

It was even thus with my master. The night he lay down his head upon his pillow of thorns, if he had waked up in hell he would not have been disappointed in the least. He felt as if he was better prepared, and only prepared, for the flames of perdition rather than the glories of heaven. I have often heard him say that this was a glorious spot for a sinner to find himself in, for then he is in a good condition to be saved.

But I see, reader, that you are anxious to become acquainted with the teacher chosen and elected at this primary school. Well, she was a near connection to the little maid who taught General Naaman, the Beauregard of that day, his first lesson. This elect lady was literally and spiritually "as a root out of dry ground" to my master. She was known as old Kitty, in the Southern country village where my master figured about this time. Her only husband, and, in fact, her first lover, was nothing but a carpenter; and who, though cradled in a manger, was afterwards a prince. They called Kitty an old maid, but this was a great mistake, as she always carried with her the witness, or rather what would be called in these days, the marriage certificate; and in her marriage ring was a beautiful white stone, on which was engraven a name which no one could read but old Kitty herself and her husband. I think this elect lady who was tutoress in this department was about four feet high, half bent over, with a little Alleghany on her back, produced by the ricketts; but she was apt to teach, and little did my master think, while strutting like a peacock in the sun light of his worldly glory, that she was to be his John the Baptist to point him to the Lamb of God, who alone could take away his sins.

Well, the school is now commenced, my master flat on his back, and the whole camp asleep except the teacher and her pupil.

"You will find, dear mourner," said she, as the voice came rifting through the curtains and fell as gentle as the dew on the attentive ear of my master, "that saving faith is one of the most common, simple and easy things in the world; just as easy as to walk into the open door of your mother's pantry when she calls you to take a piece of pie or a glass of milk which she holds in her hand."

With this and a few other child-like and simple illustrations, my master began to be seemingly all ears and eyes. Then casting his eye over the retrospective past, with its hundred and one false platforms he had erected, and the wonderful providential deliverances which he had enjoyed, he felt as if all his foundations were literally swept away; and when, like Peter, he was about up to his chin in the water, and had just time enough to stretch forth his hands and say, "Lord, save, I perish," that moment his captivity was turned back, and his mouth was filled with laughter. Although I had not seen a smile upon his face for many months, in spite of himself he now laughed so loudly as to awaken the whole encampment before he could articulate a word, and then came forth the triumphant shout of "glory to God." This was like throwing hot shot or shells into the camp, setting all on fire. This was what Peter would call "having an abundant entrance into the kingdom of God."

So much for the primary school and its teacher, and so much, and no more, for this chapter.

CHAPTER NINETEENTH.

Perhaps the peruser is anxious to know how this young babe in Christ grew after he was laid in the arms of his spiritual nurse, and how he behaved himself. Peter, you know, in speaking of these new-born babes in Christ, says that they desire the pure milk of the word that they may grow thereby. You know, also, that Malachi speaks of some that "grow up as calves in the stall." I am happy to say that this was the case with my master, as he was not put out to nurse, nor by a second-handed mother caused to draw his nourishment from a bottle. The church, or mother that travailed so long, being burdened for his soul, after his deliverance from the womb of spiritual darkness, had her breasts flowing with the pure milk of Christian love. Uncle Sam says that calves of the stall always have their noses in the pure milk. That means, he says, that converts are to every prayer meeting and class meeting, and stand up to the rack of salvation; therefore, said he, they are always ready to kill.

"You know, Dinah," says he, "when de Lor come to take dinner wid massa Abraham under de ole oak tree, while ole missa Sarah make de short cake, massa kill de fatted calf for de Lor, jus as when de prodigal son come home. De meanin ob dat be, Dinah, dat dese yer convert dat go right on, an serb de Lor good, dey is jus like de fatted calf: dey is allers ready to labor or die when de Lor he come. But de poor calf dat lib in de goose pastur, an feed on skim milk, ain't fit for de Lor, no how."

You have read the story in the old book about the poor fellow that got robbed on his way to Jericho, and was then awfully gashed up with wounds inflicted by the robbers. He was left by the roadside with just enough breath in him for life. This was about the situation of my master when Moses, with the sharp cleaver of the law, slew him. He was in a good condition to test the piety and benevolenoe of that class of christians who love mercy and care for souls.

You recollect the first one who discovered this man that lay upon the road that led from Jerusalem to Jericho, was a Levite. He was a representative then of the priesthood, and now a type of the preachers that travel all over our country. The second who came along was a Jew. He was a representative of our lay membership. Reader, this same individual is now lying, and has been for many years, midway between Jerusalem and Jericho; or in other words, both at the door of the church and the world, for the very purpose of testing the benevolence of all who profess to love their neighbor as themselves.

"The poor," says Christ, "ye have with you always, and ye may do them good whenever ye will."

These very wounds are the open doors of benevo lence, storehouses for the oil of grace, and the wine of the consolations of every good Samaritan.

Now, with your permission, I will introduce you to this subject of benevolence that has been wounded, whose tears and groans have been made in vain, as they begged for the crumbs that fall from some of your luxurious tables, and for garments from your moth eaten wardrobes. You know very well that it takes a good many members to constitute one body. Equally so the subject we have before us.

In the first place, to make up this wounded man, we will take all the slaves that have been robbed of their wives, husbands, children, liberty, the bread and water of life, and then gashed and wounded by the slaver's lash, and you have a fragment of this body. Now we bring you into an area of ten miles square, and show you ten millions of drunkards; add to them fifty millions of drunkards' wives and children, that rum and rumsellers have robbed, many of them of their religion, or hope of heaven, their property, their lives and their sacred honor.

Now behold the wounded hearts of mothers and children bleeding at every pore, and none to mollify or bind up. Listen then to the horrible shriekings as the

Delirium Tremens appears with his fetters and javelins of death; and thus you have another constituent part of the sufferer, who, Lazarus-like, lies at your doors.

Now we will go and throw a net around the inmates of licentious brothels; their name and number is legion, who once were as pure as a snow flake, and shrank from the eye of a libertine as a young dove would from the approach of the hawk.

Gather again, if you please, all the paupers from a thousand poor houses, and ten thousand hovels, in their rags and wretchedness, and unite them to the body; and this, reader, is nothing more or less than the man slain on the way to Jericho; this is the Lazarus who has starved to death at your gate.

Again we draw the curtain and introduce you to this same man in a future day, now being separated from the wealthy and selfish goats and hearken to the voice of the Judge:

"*I was an hungered, and ye gave me no meat; I was thirsty, and ye gave me no drink; I was a stranger, and ye took me not in; naked, and ye clothed me not; sick, and ye visited me not; in prison, and ye came not unto me.*"

This is an exhibition of the sympathy between the head and the body. No man can step on my little toe, way down in the mud, without at once awakening a sympathy in my head.

The church is the body of Christ, and he is their Head. No man can strike my wife without striking me at the same time, for we are one flesh. Christ is the husband of the church.

No one can abuse or neglect one of my little ones, without abusing their father; "for inasmuch, said the judge, as ye have done it unto the least of these, ye have done it unto me, their head, husband and father."

I see an affectionate father and mother with their satchels in their hands, giving the parting hand to a large family of children and servants. They are about to take a journey into a far country, and then, Christ-like, to return, perhaps in an unlooked for hour to their household. I discover in the family a poor cripple, lying on the couch; while in the cradle lies the little rose bud of the family. Now with eyes floating in tears the impress of parental lips is made upon the cheeks of those loved ones, then the parting hand is given, accompanied with the silent, choked up "farewell."

The parents now are upon the verandah. I see them turning suddenly upon their heel as if they had forgotten something of great importance. The father raises his right hand, and, elevating his fore finger, points significantly toward the poor cripple. When the eye of each child and all the servants is centered upon this subject of mercy, with flashing eye and stern voice he now breaks the awful silence. His action tends to deeply engrave upon their minds his last imperative command.

"Take heed," says he, "whatever else may be omitted, that you neglect not that helpless cripple, unless you wish to bring down upon you my wrath, whose right it is to command."

The mother's fore finger is now raised, and, pointing to the cradle, she says:

"Whatever else you may do, my children, take good care of the baby, and great shall be your reward at the return of your parents."

Even so among the last words of Christ to his shepherds and his whole household; not a word was said about caring for the D. D.s, and the healthy, wealthy and noble of the world or the church. He well knew that there would be no danger of suffering in this direction, as also did not the earthly parents at their departure from their household.

"But if," says Christ, "I find that you have neglected the suffering poor, have not visited the widow and orphan in their affliction, or have even offended one of these little ones that believe in me, then prepare your *necks* for millstones rather than your *heads* for crowns of glory."

It is very natural, when we see prisoners loaded with chains and borne off by the sheriff, to ask of what offence the prisoner was guilty. Now, we enquire for the crime of those millions of goats, borne off by the tormenters under the sentence of the judge, "Depart, ye cursed." Let the sacred pages answer: Their crime was doing nothing; or rather, neglecting to care for Christ's little ones, "The least," said he, "of these, my brethren." Dives, come up here with your red hot chains! What was the black catalogue of your crimes, murder, theft, adultery, fornication, drunkenness, or the whole catalogue compounded?

"Oh, no," he exclaims, with scalding tears, "it was that fashionable, popular sin of the day. I simply neglected a poor man who lay at my gate, begging in vain for the crumbs that fell from my luxurious banqueting board. Selfishness was my predominant sin; one," says he, "that is populating hell very fast in 1860."

Alas! alas! what a fashionable, common and deceptive sin is this! How awfully disappointed were these well fed goats, as they simultaneously exclaimed,

"When saw we the Lord destitute and suffering? If we had known that thou hadst been a bishop, or presiding elder, some professor or doctor of divinity, the folding doors of our parlors would have been thrown wide open, our table would have been spread with the luxuries of life and the dainties of the season. We never dreamed that such an illustrious personage cared for the despised sons and daughters of Ham, the wretched subjects of rum, the Mary Magdalenes, the despised poor in their rags. We little dreamed that this was the robbed and wounded man spoken of in the Gospel, whom we looked at, opened his pocket-book, found destitute of money, and learning that he did not belong to our church, but was nothing but a nigger, drunkard, harlot or pauper, wished him well, and passed on as did the church member."

Great God! what will be the disappointment of such ministers and members, whose false hopes have brought them to the very gates of heaven, but who, like Capernaum, have been thrust down to hell, while harlots and publicans, washed in the blood of the Lamb, whom they would hardly touch, unless with a pair of tongs, in the day of their probation, are entering by millions through the pearly gates, and are crowned.

I have often been with my present master to conferences, and other ministerial assemblages. The venerable bishop, in the act of solemn ordination, would propound many solemn questions to the candidate, among which is the following:

"Wilt thou diligently search for the poor in your charge or circuit, to comfort and bless them?"

The answer is:

"I will do so, the Lord being my helper."

At that moment an ejaculatory prayer would be uttered by my master.

"O Lord, help them to carry out their ordination vows when they get to their charges."

I have been gratified to see that some of them do pay their vows to the Most High God, while I have been astonished and distressed at others, who seem to regard such a vow as written upon the sand or snow. Their searches after the poor on their charges make me think of my present master, who, when a young man, lost his right eye in consequence of intense inflammation, which burst the ball and mingled the contents with the waters of the Blue Juniatta. This eye, now being much disfigured, an occulist inserted an artificial glass eye, which was so arranged on the muscles that it would move and roll in its orbit precisely like the natural eye, and scarce any one, without close inspection, would detect this fashionable lie, as it was in appearance so nearly like the other. My master's eyes were now much like those of the Pharisee and those of a true Christian. While one seeing, perceived not, the other was an avenue that filled his body full of light.

But you are asking for the comparison. Well, I will tell you that my master was not made up altogether of such unfeeling materials as railroad timbers, iron, spikes, &c. He always had a very tender regard for the society of ladies, and I always observed that when he promenaded with them he would always manage to keep the best eye next to the object of his affections.

I have noticed also, that some of these ministers when they came out from under their ordination vows, and had gone to their charges, would in their searches for the poor in their wretched cabins, unfortunately have these cabins on the side of their glass eye; while their best eye would dilligently search out the two storied fronts; and land them, almost hurry them upon soft spring cushioned sofa, when they would gracefully pat and pet the dear children of the wealthy brother and sister, while the innocent chickens would be losing their heads, preparatory to a sumptuous dinner.

They could not, of course, be blamed for passing by the poor, as they were always situated on the blind side. All the difference in these ministers is this, one like the good samaritan, looks up the poor; the other, overlooks the poor, that is all. Oh Lord! how fashionable, how common and damning is this sin of overlooking the poor.

St. James hangs all such professors on a gallows fifty cubits high. "Have not the faith of our Lord Jesus Christ," says he, "the Lord of glory, with respect to persons, for if there comes into your assembly a man having on a gold ring and in gay clothing; and there also comes in a poor man in vile clothing; and ye have respect to him that weareth the gay clothing, and say unto him, sit thou here in a good place; and say to the poor, stand thou there, or sit here under my footstocl, are ye not partial and convinced of the Law of transgressors?"

We understand the apostle to say, that whosoever shall keep the whole law, even if there should be a thousand items, and we should keep strictly nine hundred and ninety-nine, and yet be guilty of the sin of "respect" or "partiality" unto persons, we are as surely damned as there is an impartial God sitting on the throne.

If the chain let down for David into the horrible pit, had been made of a thousand links, and one link only of the whole, in consequence of a flaw, had broken, he would have gone back to the bottom, though he had been within a foot of the top. A CHAIN IS NO STRONGER THAN ITS WEAKEST LINK, and woe to the man whose hopes of heaven are hanging on a broken link, i. e.; keeping just as many commandments as suits his convenience. I do believe, rag though I am, that this sin of popular churches is doing much to colonize the nether pit of woe.

Although my master had been converted to the Methodists, when a small boy, still in order to be saved he found it necessary to be afterwards converted to God. Notwithstanding I have somewhat against him, not that he ever fell an inch from his first love; but I am sorry to say that for two or three years he was a miserable pro-slavery, pro-whiskey, pro-fessor; although a tee-totaler in his own personal habits. Yet he had no sense of condemnation from God, as he walked up to the light of those dark days; at least so far as it glimmered upon these two subjects of reform. He was then a child. He thought, spoke and understood as a child; but in about two and a half years after his spiritual birth, he arrived to the full stature of a man, in Christ. He put away childish things.— He had proved the truth of the ancient adage: "They who lie down with dogs will get up with fleas." When the young medical student enters the dissecting room, he fancies the dead bodies around him to be ghosts, grinning upon him from every corner of the room.— But after a long experience with death and the charnel house, he feels no more terror than when in a butcher's stall. So

> "Vice is a monster of such frightful mean,
> That to be dreaded, needs but to be seen,
> When we become familiar with its face,
> From loathing, pity; and from that embrace."

The tender mother will thumb the little harmless *nit* on the hair of her flaxen headed boy, for she knows full well that in twenty-four hours it will be a great grandfather. Now if these sins, like the nits of my comparison, had by the former shepherds been crushed while young, our entire country would have been vocal with praises to God. My master, during his fourteen years' experience upon public works, had given his workmen perhaps ten thousand dollars worth of whiskey, in jiggers, as they were called. He thus became familiar with drunkenness, and being in the midst of slavery, 'tis no wonder that he became familiar with the *fleas* and *vermin* on those two dogs. Strange, and wonderful to relate, that such cardinal sins could not have been seen, and hated by the church in 1840, as they are now in 1861. My master in those days only saw "men as trees walking," but when the great eye-opener gave him the second touch, and he saw himself in the sunlight; every flea had a writ of ejectment served upon him, as a usurper on the plantation, and he learned the difference between *Compromising* and *destroying* the works of the Devil.

CHAPTER TWENTIETH.

Reader mine: We have had rather a long and serious time in the old laboratory, or dissecting office, as we have been taking to pieces my blind master, in search of some of the plague spots of sin which dwelt within him. Be of good cheer, for we have but one or two more spots to purify, and then we will put this town clock together again, oil the wheels, and see to it that both pointers stand perpendicular at twelve o'clock, neither too slow nor too fast. It is sad enough for an individual to be deceived by his watch, as he finds himself just five minutes behind the time, puffing and blowing, with his baggage in his hands, hearing the old locomotive mock him as its whistle warns all off the track at the remotest point of vision. 'Tis very unpleasant to hear the steamboat bell tapping, stroke after stroke, just out of the harbor, as much as to say:

"Good bye, laziness."

But in the case of the watch there is but an individual disappointment or suffering. On the other hand, if the town clock goes wrong, all the clocks and watches in the city, which are set by it, are wrong also; unless we except those dumb watches which have no heart or works, but are like some preachers and politicians, who turn their hands on the dial to suit the time of their neighbor's watch, one after another, as they pass on the sidewalk; or are found in a house well furnished, before the face of a clock whose time may help in *personal popularity*, and to each of whom, as they turn the hands, will exclaim,

"Our time, I see, agrees; and my watch never kept any different time from yours, and if it has seemed at any time to vary, the fault was not in the watch, but in the inability of the reporter to decipher the figures on the dial."

Hence, all watches which are thus wound, capable of being wound round and round, backwards or forwards at pleasure, without marring something, must have a good deal of India rubber somewhere. But India rubber makes good kindling wood, as thousands now in perdition know full well.

Town clocks should be perfectly reliable, or every watch or clock that is set to their time is a liar also; a liar to themselves as well as to others.

Watchmen on the walls of Zion are town clocks, and all eyes are looking to them for an example in every good work and doctrine. "If the blind lead the blind, both shall fall into the ditch," and in my experience for many years I have found the old proverb literally true: "Like priest, like people; like shepherd, like flock." Oh, how necessary that every wheel in this town clock be purified in the blood of the Lamb, and every wheel oiled with the grace of life, that they may make true time, point out the hours and minutes, with their duties, lest those who look upon give them up as false guides, and the infidels laugh them to scorn. Or, to use the language of the Holy Ghost, that after they have been sanctified wholly, soul, body and spirit, that they be kept unblamable unto the appearing of the Lord; proving at the same time, the faithfulness of him who had called them to do these things for them.

I have often been with my master in some strange pulpit, when the preacher in charge would very politely introduce him to the congregation as a "blind preacher," which my master would playfully yet flatly deny.

"I acknowledge," says he, "that I am a blind man, but not a blind preacher. A blind preacher is one of the greatest curses to a community that could well be thought of. Jesus Christ never sent forth a blind guide to bring his people home."

But we must hasten to the purification of this single spot before we invite our friends to assist us in raising the building.

The doctrine which my master now loves and preaches is, that when a person is soundly converted to God, that moment he is sanctified and made an heir of heaven, as truly as was Enoch at the time of his translation. As the infant, at the death of its father, claims an equal proportion of the estate with the adult brothers and sisters. He believes, also, that God never had an unsanctified or unholy child in his family, and that seldom, if ever, a child was born of the Spirit that was sanctified wholly at its birth, or had perfected that holiness which was commenced at the time of birth. He believes there is a point of time in this life when those graces are perfected, as much as was the Ark at the beginning of the deluge; or as the finished stones at the building of the Temple; as there was not heard the sound of the ax or hammer on the Ark, or a polishing chisel on the goodly stones of the Temple, as they came together.

At my master's conversion, he was in about the same condition *spiritually* as was Lazarus *naturally* after he was brought to life and crept out of the cave, he had his grave clothes wrapped around him, and a napkin over his eyes, and his feet and hands were tied, until Christ spake the second time:

"Loose him, and let him go."

Then he was free indeed. It was with my master, as I believe is generally the case with young converts who are brought from death to life, as really *spiritually* as Lazarus was literally or *naturally*. But they are far from being free indeed. Their hands and feet are tied with the silken cords of pride, vain glory, self-righteousness, &c., &c.

Christ is the only one who left his grave clothes behind him when he came forth from the sepulchre. But it is not so with young converts, especially those deeply rooted in sin. They bring out with them many besetments; they speak a broken language, partly their native tongue. They also have a napkin of unbelief over their eyes.

An occulist dare not open the blind eye suddenly to the meridian light, but several layers of cloth are hung before its vision, which are taken off one by one, as the patient can bear it, until he can look at the morning sun fair in the face, under a cloudless sky. This places him in a land of Beulah, far beyond Doubting Castle, his sun and moon, unless he backslides, going no more down.

The spot we have under examination on the Christian character of my master, was the napkin of unbelief in the doctrine of "perfect love, or an entire sanctification," or, what is called by Wesley and his followers, the "second blessing." The first two or three years of his Christian life he rather ridiculed the doctrine, but a God of mercy winked at it as a childhood ignorance and foolishness, for "as the old cock crows, the young cocks learn." So he learned from Judaizing teachers, who themselves are ever learning, but never able to come to the knowledge of the truth, at least of this glorious truth. They creep into houses with their unhallowed leaven, and instead of leading out of darkness, rather lead many silly women and children into the fog upon this subject.

This we also set down as one of the popular sins of the day, and one which brings blight and mildew upon the goodly heritage.

But I must hasten to my master's experience upon

[60]

this subject, for all true knowledge and light is the result of heartfelt experience. The Devil can rob any Christian of almost any jewel but this. This is his sheet anchor in the storm; this alone will qualify him as a witness in any court, either in heaven or earth. But the moistened clay that the great eye-opener used as he lifted the eyelid of faith in his soul, and so filled his whole body full of light on this subject, was another "root out of dry ground," about another match for aunt Kitty, his first spiritual nurse. It was old Father Hawbecker, a Dutch local preacher of the "United Brethren's Society," in Pennsylvania. He was a poor man, and a butcher by trade. He wore patches on his knees, which, by the by, is not a bad recommendation for a minister of the Gospel.

He knew but little about philosophy or astronomy, but he could dive as deeply as any man I ever knew into "the sea of glass," and when he got into the old gospel diving bell, he could bring up rich gems, and sparkling diamonds that even Infidels could but admire as holiness, like a lighted candle, or sparkling diamond will manifest its beauty and worth to the most advantage in dark and benighted regions. It was known all over the country, among saints and sinners, that old daddy Hawbecker, who had not in all probability seen the outside of a College, professed to be holy; to have been made perfect in love, and insisted upon it that every man and woman that sinned was of the Devil; and while all acknowledged his goodness and holy example, and would send for him, far and near, in the straits of a dying hour; yet he was generally numbered among the silly fools in the juvenile class of my master, who could scarcely spell "Bag," as a foolish old fanatic. Among these were many who are gracing modern pulpits, fresh from the College at Athens, with their diplomatic sheep-skins in one hand, and their sheep-shears in the other, saying to some wealthy flock, "what is the prospect for wool here?"

Here is another fashionable sin for which God is cursing the churches. The supporting and giving God-speed to such hirelings, with high salaries, who have never been baptized at Jerusalem, or any where else; while a still larger class are cursed for withholding their support from the consecrated shepherds of the flock; said Paul to his Corinthian brethren, "for ye see your calling brethren, how that not many wise, not many mighty, not many noble are called. But God hath chosen the foolish things of this world, to confound the wise; and the weak things of the world, to confound the things that are mighty; and base things of this world, and things which are despised hath God chosen; yea, and things which are not, to bring to nought things that are," giving as a reason, "that no flesh should glory in his presence."

Alas! what a deceptive practice it is, to prepare a beautiful pot of odor, both in the pulpit and gallery, which is enjoyed only by the preacher and the singers, while the cloud of incense never rises higher than that from the offering of Cain. Singing and preaching to once's self exclusively, and for one's own glory, is to waken the jealousy of the Lord, who has declared that he will not give his glory to another.

Such worshipers will knock in vain at the door where the marriage supper of the Lamb is celebrated. Oh, what a deceptive, damning sin is this! But I am tempted to give you, by way of an anchovy the religious experience of this hay-mow Doctor of Divinity in his own language, which was the foundation on which he commenced building his spiritual house:

" Mein bredren, ven I vas to vork for mine masther 'pout forty years ago, I t'inks I bees von poor miserable sinner, an' I shall goes to hell. Den I feels so pad I cannot eat—I cannot shleep; so I goes out to te parn, and I brays so loud an' hart as I can, and I feels no petter yet, py an' py mine masther comes out an' say, "Shacop, you musht shtop! you vill kill yourself."—Put I says, "I cannot shtop! I musht have rest to my soul!" Den mein sisther comes out an' tells me to get up, I shall kill myself; put I dells her, "I shall not sthop, for I musht have rest to my soul!"

Den I goes up onto de hay, an' I brays an' brays all night, an' ven de morning light comes in, I feels *God* did convert my soul; and I shump up an' shlaps my hans, an' cries, "Clory to *Cot!*" Den I says, "O! mein *Cot* —I vants everypody to haf dis coot relishion; an I tinks vere shall I go first? So I tinks I vill go to de shoemaker's, an tell him all apout it. So I tinks I vill go an get mein poots, an take 'em down an get 'em mended, and dat vill pe a coot vay to pegin to talk mit him. So ven I has got shtarted I tinks de *Spirit* say to me:

"Shacop, vot you doin mit your poots? You don't care apout gettin dem mended—vat den does you vant de shoemaker to tink you comes to get de poots mended, ven you pees only goin to talk apout de relishion!"

Den I says, "O! mein *Cot*, I has not got de relishion 'nough yet." Den I goes right back to de parn an I prays an prays all night, and den de *Lort* gif me de sanctification! and den I could go midout mein poots, an tell de man vat I cum for—to talk apout de relishion; and not make pelief I vants my poots mended, ven dat ain't vat I cum for."

Here is another fashionable sin of the day; it is a mock modesty. Instead of going to sinners as an honest physician would go to the bedside of his languishing patient, and while feeling his pulse, plainly declare to him that, without sudden relief, immediate death is inevitable; if the devil can get us to take our boots in our hand when we talk to sinners, he knows full well that it will neutralize all of our exhortations and warnings. Jesus Christ and the apostles, when they raised their warning voices with their tearful eyes, impressed the sinner full well that they were in earnest, and they left their flocks trembling.

The arrow that flies like lightning and is driven to the feather, springs from a well bent and vigorous bow. But when ministers or members talk, pray, or preach with a milk and water zeal, the Devil will whisper in that sinner's ears at the same time, "That fellow does not half believe his own preaching," and they may blow around Jericho until they superannuate and die, without starting the mortar on the outside of the enemy's wall. But Daddy Hawbecker felt more like Moses, and leaving his boots or shoes behind him, he would place his naked feet on the rock, and thus God made him a sweet savor of life unto life in the awakening of my master to the subject of holiness; and he, after sweeping about six months, like the woman spoken of in the Gospel, at last found the full amount of coin. I think it was in the morning, but then I will open the family Bible as it lies before me, and take an extract, as it is recorded on the family record, of both the natural and spiritual births of my master and his family, day and date, as they were brought in by nature and grace. Here, then, is the record:

George Whitmore Henry, born January 6th, 1801.

Born again, of the water and Spirit, August 10th, 1842, at one o'clock A. M.

Sanctified wholly, soul, body and spirit, September 5th, 1845.

No one, I suppose, even Nicodemus himself, will doubt the natural birth of my master, while many will stumble at the spiritual record, of which I am glad that their unbelief does not affect the witness. I have often heard my master say that if his friends will engrave anything upon his tombstone, let it be the above extract from the family Bible. But I must hasten to the testimony and the close of this first volume.

On the 5th of September, 1845, a camp-meeting was in session in Herkimer county, N. Y. About five o'clock in the morning was the hour when it was appointed that Brother Gorham should preach upon the subject of holiness. At about half past four he mounted the stand, and, in concert with an English robin that was perched upon a bough, began to sing that gentle melody,

"Glory to the Lamb."

This at once brought the slumbering Israel upon their feet, and very soon they were up and dressed, and, seated before the altar, were swelling the song on that calm, lovely and never to be forgotten morning. My master, I recollect, seemed to be fairly swept out of bed as if by a wave of glory. His mouth was filled with laughter, and his cheeks flowed down with tears of joy. The scene was similar to that when he crossed the threshhold of the kingdom of grace. He was so happy that I saw it was with great difficulty that he could tie his shoes, for on this occasion, you will remember that I was warming and comforting the body of my master, not having then been worn so as to be cast off with the rags. I was, therefore, an eye-witness to the subject of which I am now relating. Jeremy Taylor, when touching the subject of extremes, said, that Moses, while rebuking Aaron for breaking one commandment, broke ten himself; and that the Lord at one time was not able to communicate a message to Isaiah in consequence of the young prophet's being in a state of extatic glory and beatific vision, until he was soothed down by singing. It was about so with my master, as

> "Small draughts intoxicate the brain,
> But drinking largely sobers us again."

Well, my master soon found himself seated before the sanctuary, where the honey dropped freely into his soul from the Rock, while brother Gorham was pointing out the right and the wrong ways to attain a state of holiness. No man would employ a pilot to guide his vessel through the straits who had not first been through himself and become familiar with the passage, and so be able to return and pilot others. It was so with brother Gorham. He had, like Caleb and Joshua, crossed over himself, and had returned with his grapes and pomegranates to pilot on the sacramental hosts of God's elect to the good in the promised land. While Daddy Hawbecker was the eye-salve of clay, brother Gorham seemed to be the Bethesday of washing. My master now began to look steadfastly into heaven, and to gather up the promises which abounded on the subject of holiness; and spread them out before the Lord just as a man would lay bank bills upon the counter, and demand from the cashier the amount in gold and silver, with a determination never to leave the bank until every bill was honored with the specie which its face demanded.

Now, reader, let us leave our master at the counter of the bank while you go with me to a hydropathic institution for an illustration of what is to follow.

In spending a week at this establishment, where the packing, ducking, plunging and sitting baths were going on, there was one place they called the douche. There was a large reservoir of water sitting upon the roof of a large three storied building. The candidate for this operation, after being divested of all his clothing, was placed immediately at the mouth of a conduit of water, which fell about forty feet with tremendous power on the patient, he, to accomplish all this, simply pulling a wire and raising a valve.

My master had often, previous to this, felt the gentle dews and copious showers of grace upon his heart, but he now stood with his naked soul beneath this heavenly laver, and faith got hold of a wire which raised the valve of full salvation. Now a water-spout of grace seemed to strike him upon the head, as if at first to purify every pigeon hole in his brain of every stain of unbelief, and then downwards to the end of his toes. If it had been literal, he says, it would not have been more sensible. My master then fell like a bullock at the slaughter. Though often slain before, and perhaps a hundred times since, this was the only time but what he was perfectly sensible of the operations of the spirit within him, and to hear and know all that was said and going on about him. But while he now laid on the ground, his outer ear was perfectly sealed to the voice of the preacher or any human voice. But the Holy Ghost now beareth witness that there was a voice which spake seemingly audibly to his interior ear, saying:

"What do you want this blessing for?"

To which my master replied, that he might "be better qualified to preach the Gospel." At that moment surge after surge of the spirit, like the ebbing and flowing of the sea, seemed to course through every vein, nerve and marrow of the entire man, and I have often heard my master say that it seemed as if the whole building was coming to pieces.

The next question propounded to him by the Spirit was:

"Will you preach entire holiness in the village of Frankfort?" which was a very wicked place where he was now living. To which my master replied, "Yea, Lord," when immediately the same surging operation went through the entire man. During this scene, which occupied probably about ten minutes, my master says he was without joy, but rather, like Moses, did exceedingly fear and quake. But when this last surging passed away, his outer ear was unstopped, and he again heard the voice of the preacher, the shouts of the redeemed, the singing of birds, and in a moment after stood erect and leaped from the dissecting-board, bidding good bye to the dead; something like the corpse that the Jews laid in the coffin of the prophet Elisha, after he had been dead fifty years. The moment the corpse touched the bones he came to life, leaped from the coffin, and at once buckled on his sword for the war.

Oh, the flood of heavenly joy that permeated at once his whole soul! How beggarly is human language to express such heavenly felicity and rapture experienced in full redemption! No recording angel, by dipping his pen in the ink-horn of salvation, can write it.

Ask young Isaiah how he felt after the burning coal was placed upon his lips; ask David what made him feel like running through a troop and leaping over a wall; enquire of St. Paul how he felt when he was caught up to the third heavens; ask John Bunyan, the Baptist, and Payson, the Presbyterian, how they felt when they entered the land of Beulah; and they will, with one accord, tell you that individual experience alone can reveal this heaven-born truth, this panacea for the carnal mind.

"My brethren, I have found a land that doth abound
With food as sweet as manna;
The more I eat, I find the more I am inclined
To shout, and sing Hosanna.
My soul now longs to go where I shall fully know
The glories of my Saviour,
And while I go along I'll sing my happy song,
I hope to live forever."

Amen, Hallelujah!

And now, with this, we will bid my fifth master good bye, and calling upon "Happy John" will be our first business in the next chapter. Thus much, and no more.

Kind Reader, adieu.

[71]

MY SIXTH MASTER.

CHAPTER TWENTY-FIRST.

LIFE OF HAPPY JOHN.

Hallo! here lies a Lazarus at our gate, all covered with whisky sores, without a dog to lick his wounds, bruised and mangled by the fall, begging not only for crumbs, but also rags for bandages, and plasters to bind up his putrid sores; and, without respect to the honorable position I had gained while serving my five previous masters, starting, as I did, from the dust of South Carolina, and gradually rising to the sunlit hills in the land of Beulah, my mistress, as a reward for warming the back of her blind husband for years, rent me in pieces, like Joseph's coat, and handed me over to this Bacchanalian prince.

So, now, reader, you find your old acquaintance, the honorable Tell Tale Rag, at once reduced, as you think, to a very mean and dishonorable calling. But yesterday I was folded in the bureau drawer of my mistress, without spot or wrinkle, resting from my labors, consoling myself that I had finished my work on earth. After all, although made into a sticking plaster, was I ever doing more good, or entitled to greater honor, than I am now, ministering comfort to the afflicted. Honor and glory, whose whole soul, body and spirit is not made up of entire goodness, is all vanity — a mere soap bubble. Is Abraham Lincoln any better man while sitting in the chair of state, than when he was earning that honorable cognomen of "Honest Abe," while splitting rails at the old homestead? We trow not. Did Jesus Christ ever occupy one position more honorable or elevated than another? If he did, it was when he was binding up the broken-hearted, and descending into horrible pits, to get his arms beneath the soul and body of drunkards and harlots. Even so, I am comforted while comforting others. Moreover, I will make a speculation out of my new position. Was there ever a better place to take notes in short hand of the sorrows that befell my new and sixth master, and to magnify the grace of God, who, as the sequel will show, snatched him from the very gates of hell and plunged him into the river of life, and set him among his princes, and made him the happiest man, perhaps, in all Western New York, insomuch that he is called, by saint and sinner, instead of Agar Hall, Happy John. And now, dear reader,

I am to give you a sketch of his life, perfectly unvarnished, as it fell from his lips in 1861, while walking with God in the land of Beulah. As to his visions and views of the future world, you are at perfect liberty to place any estimate, or make any comment thereon you please. And so shall the writer and reader render account to God in the great day.

Agar Hall was born in the north of England, in the county of Cumberland, in the parish of Oldstone, on the fourth of January, 1803. His parents were irreligious; but notwithstanding Agar was well instructed in the Sabbath School, he having gained a high prize in his class, from the Superintendent, when he was fourteen years of age. He says the Holy Spirit continually strove with him to look to Christ for salvation while his heart was tender, before the evil day of old age should harden his heart and whiten his locks; but the wicked one, he says, set him to looking at the variety of sects and denominations. Therefore, instead of being fed, as a babe of Christ, on the sweet and flowing milk of the Gospel, the adversary of his soul began to feed the simple-hearted youth on the imperfections of religious professors, as turkey buzzards feed their young on putrifaction. Thus the youthful furrows of Agar's heart were sown with tares, and, as the sequel will show, they produced an abundant crop. He said he thought some of the Methodists had religion, while others, he believed, were hypocrites. Satan also made him believe that, if he embraced religion, he must bid a final farewell to all the joys and pleasures of this world, and that sorrow and deep gloom, a chapfallen countenance, with a head bowed as a bulrush, was the legacy of the children and heirs of the King of Kings.

Alas! what a common, fashionable and deceptive lie. Every page of Holy Writ sparkles with promises, like stars in the milky way, to cheer the youth, gladden his heart, and brighten his eye with the sweet hopes of heaven, while millions of living witnesses, of Christian pilgrims with hearts full of heavenly joy, both living and dying, have proved this old destroyer to be the father of lies.

On the 17th of July, 1818, Agar left England with his father and mother and five of his younger brothers and sisters, and landed at Quebec on the second of September. Agar says that, in the midst of the mountainous waves, driven by the storm-king, while crossing the Atlantic, his youthful heart was equally agitated, as the fear of death brooded over him, and the Holy Ghost rent the vail of the future. This brought the youth trembling upon his knees, but when the sea was calm, his heart and conscience were again rocked to sleep in the cradle of carnal security, and his solemn promises to God, as if written upon the sand, were swept away as with a deluge of deceitful mirth, so natural and common to youth.

And now we pass over many eventful scenes, and find Agar and his father's family in Rochester, New York, in 1820, where he spent many years of his life, until 1861, in which year he dictates this narrative. Agar further says that, when he came to Rochester, he was a good, honest and industrious lad; that is, if we measure him in Cæsar's half bushel, or weigh him in the world's moral balance: just good enough to miss of heaven, if death had suddenly brought him to the gates of pearl, over which is written, in letters of living light, "Nothing entereth here that defileth, or that has not been born again of the incorruptible seed."

Agar was now eighteen years old — the most uncontrolable period in the history of young men, and about fifteen, the most dangerous to young ladies. Like poultry, the most tender period of their life is when they are about pin-feathering — when they are changing from a silly gosling to a goose. Even so, young men and women, when they are changing from girl to womanhood and from boy to manhood: they are wiser, in their own estimation, than father or mother, and it is very humiliating for these young coxcomb dignitaries to be controlled by their mother, or the old woman, as they sometimes term her. They are like young bees, the largest when first hatched out. At this period in the epoch of young men and women, is where two roads meet, and where millions gradually switch off from the path of virtue into the slimy, serpentine labyrinth of drunkenness, licentiousness, and a thousand snares of the wicked one, and unless Almighty Grace is suffered to get her arms of mercy beneath them and lift them up, their uncontrolable lusts will bind their souls and bodies in fetters of brass, and cast them over the cliff of time, and one splash on the lake of fire and brimstone will do that which the Gospel, the prayers and tears of their friends fail to do, namely, to arouse them to a sense of their guilt and danger, until they find themselves, instead of prisoners of hope, prisoners of despair, and all the difference there is between a sinner on earth and a sinner in hell is, the former is lost with a remedy, and the latter is lost without a remedy.

But we will go back to the switch where the youthful Agar, our "young America," first began to nibble at the seductive bait which concealed a hook of hell, on the end of a line of the destroyer of millions, under the cognomen of King Alcohol, who reigned in him and reigned over him, until destruction, as the sequel will show, had about finished up her work, and left him a subject for the oil and wine of the good Samaritan.

The first business of our youthful Agar was to take

up the spade on the Clinton ditch, or the grand Erie Canal, on the bosom of whose waters is now bearing the breadstuffs of the great West and exchanging it for the spices and luxuries of the East. But, alas! while this has proved a blessing to the world, how many mother's sons have taken their first drink of whisky as they broke the first sod, and never quit until caged in a prison, or handed over by the delirium tremens to the sexton, a bloated drunkard, to lay in a newly dug or untimely grave. And perhaps it would not be extravagant if we should say that the rum, mingled with tears, flowing down the bloated cheek of the sons of Bacchus, together with the tears wrung out of the hearts of parents, children and friends, in consequence thereof, we say, would it not fill the banks of the old Erie with its fire waters?

As it was a common rule among contractors to empty as many whisky barrels as they did flour barrels, while a good share of the laborer's hard wages was spent in the diving holes of these slime pits of Sodom, which are now legalized and tolerated by those chosen public guardians of the morals, both of city-full and country-waste, a protection that vultures give to lambs. This is one of the popular, fashionable sins of the day.

But the canal is not to bear all this burden of iniquity. Oh, no! Agar had this terrible poison pressed to his lips by a father's hand, while sinking wells with him, and other like business, in and about the city of Rochester. Great God! is it not enough that fathers should commit a whisky suicide, and with their own hands, prematurely open the gates of eternity, and, like a surprise party, enter the regions of the damned before the devils expected them, and when there, in vain call for some Lazarus to return to earth to warn that son of his to dash to the ground the very cup of death which a father's hand had pressed so often to the pure lips of his youthful son?

Alas! what tormentors will be the children of wicked parents, who have followed in the wake of their example, who, with scorpion fingers, shall charge home upon them one great cause of their damnation. But, reader, we are persuaded of better things, touching the history of the father and son of whom we now write. The father of Agar died on the 25th of April, 1826, and during the year that pale consumption caused him to spit up his vitals and steal away his flesh by the ounce, Thomas Hall, the father of Agar, found both place and space to repent, made peace with God, lost the fear of death, and, through rich abounding grace, his sun went down under a cloudless sky. Great grief and melancholy then seized the heart of Agar, and, instead of falling upon his knees before Him who bindeth up the broken-hearted, he opened his mouth still wider for the sop, and, as that went in torrents down, the Devil floated down with it; and, instead of standing in the breach made by death, as a good son and elder brother, to comfort a widowed mother, with a young brood of orphans, rum transformed this once good boy, this hope of a fond mother, into the very devil of devils. A mother's tears and persuasions, in connection with other friends, seemed to be like throwing brimstone to augment the flames of hell. Rum and rumsellers soon made him a match for the ancient demoniacs, walking among the tombs, that no chains could bind, or the tears, prayers or arguments could persuade.

The Southern turkey buzzard, early in the morning, will snuff, at the distance of many miles, the rotten carcase of some old horse, and, during the day, they will luxuriate on the putrefaction, and return, at night, to their rookery with a full crop; and as it is against the law to kill them, as they are considered beneficial to the health of the city, in consequence of their licking up the filth of the streets, therefore they become very tame and domesticated, and whenever they are plagued or crossed, as they are sometimes by the boys, they will at once open wide their filthy mouths, and cast up, on the pavement or floor, all the rottenness and filth they have gathered during the day.

'T was even so with this now bloated child of Bacchus. Early in the morning he would emerge from his mother's log cabin, and, like the buzzard, begin to snuff the distant rum-hole, where he would glut himself in that which was worse than carrion, and then swagger through the streets, and whoever crossed his path, like the buzzard, he would disgorge his filth upon them in blasphemous oaths and filthy talk, that would make the whole Five Points blush with shame. And this was the only provision and comfort that this terrible child would bear home, night after night, and month after month, to this disconsolate household. One time, Agar says, his mother and sister mixed in his jug a dose of Dr. Chambers' medicine, which caused him almost to vomit himself up. But this only served to stir up his wrath, and make room for a still larger dose. The dog turned again to his own vomit. His friends then forbid the rumsellers giving him liquor, but this was like preaching repentance to a Pharisee. They would still deal out more. Sometimes his friends would break his bottles. Oft has he been picked up by them at midnight, from the cold earth, stupefied with rum and chilled to the vitals by the frosts of the wintry night. He was now about ready to graduate in the alcoholic school. He entered the class of delirium tremens. This not only destroyed the peace, but turned his mother's household into a bedlam, and disturbed the whole community. Honest and quiet neighbors must be called in, by night and by day, to bind this rum-fiend, and prevent his wicked hands from breaking the head as well as the heart of an affectionate mother. After being partially restored by the aid of Dr. Coleman, and receiving his Christian advice and warning voice, he went forth again and plunged still deeper into sin, until he had passed through the horrors of eighteen fits of the delirium tremens; and, in order to augment the horrors of those awful deliriums, all hell seemed to furnish and crowd his room with damned ghosts, hissing serpents, filthy toads and crawling worms, seemingly vibrating, like a pendulum, over the very threshhold of the gate of hell. During the struggle of the eighteenth fit, Dr. Wright, of Rochester, drew forth his watch, and said to the horror-stricken group, that stood gazing in breathless silence, that if that delirium fiend did not relinquish his hold within forty seconds, the unfortunate victim must pass away to reap the harvest his own hands had sown broadcast, and meet a drunkard's reward. But just at that awful moment, two sweet sisters came rushing in, whose names, we afterwards learned, were Grace and Mercy, and they snatched this brand from the burning, and plunged him into a pool hard by the sheep market, known as Bethesda. This quenched the violence of the alcoholic flame for a season, and friends fondly hoped a reformation would then begin. But, alas! it was a forlorn hope. When Agar's health was so restored that he was able to labor, unfortunately for him, and wicked and unmerciful were his neighbors and acquaintances, who would not give him employment.

At this crisis, the devil sent an old drunken Englishman from Canada, who had just change enough to buy one jug of whisky, which he pressed to the lips of Agar, and which soon laid him again in the gutter of infamy, from which he arose, and, with his rum chum, turned his back upon the city of Rochester, and with a serpentine route, they staggered and swaggered, drinking, cursing and swearing. In 1829, the city of Kingston, Upper Canada, was honored with a grand entrance of these two distinguished sons of Bacchus. From their regalia, their blooming cheeks and noses, and their eyelids bound with red ferreting, together with their very conversation and breath, would declare at once, to any stranger, their pedigree, their royal blood, legitimate children of his royal majesty, King Alcohol. From Kingston they went to Long Falls, and engaged in working on the Riden canal. But here they found a restrictive temperance law. No hand was allowed to have but three drinks, or giggers, a day, which were given him by his employer, while the laborer was not suffered to purchase and drink, in addition, but one quart a day, on the penalty of being discharged. This law so strapped down the dignity and liberties of Johnny Bull, Agar's Bacchanalian chum, that he seceded and left the canal, raised the palmetto flag, and returned to his old homestead, near Toronto, where, in his palmy days, he had a fine farm, a gristmill and distillery, all of which he long since had swallowed, and, soon after he returned, he laid down his bloated carcase in an untimely grave.

But we will now return to the canal and enquire after our friend, Agar. Well, here we find him, with his bundle in his hand, Cain-like, fleeing from the wrath of the Catholics, whom he had unmercifully lacerated with his abusive tongue, which had been set on fire of hell, fearing, he said, they would take his life sometime as he lay senseless in the gutter. A place called Edwards' Rapids, on the canal, is now graced with our hero, where he continued for nearly two years. Awful to relate, the scenes, the suffering horrors that accompanied him during his sojourn here. It would require the pen of an archangel, dipping it in the gall of bitterness, to describe, whose watchful eye oft saw him at midnight, with all his faculties bound in fetters of brass, while his tattered garments were cemented by the hoary frosts to the ice-bound earth, friendless and homeless, far from a mother's watchful eye and soft hand, that used to press the cordial to the feverish lips, to one so often dandled on the lap of parental love. But, instead thereof, Agar says, scores of damned ghosts and hellish fiends, plainly visible, would flock around him, causing his bloated flesh to quiver on his bones as if the flames of hell had seized upon him. Agar was now precisely like the man spoken of in the Gospel, that lay between Jericho and Jerusalem: robbed by the thievish rumseller of every thing that should make life desirable, while sin, that sting of death, made visible many gaping wounds in his precious soul. But there was an eye which never slumbereth, beheld in that half putrid frame, in that dilapidated casket, a jewel more valuable than all earth's treasures, that cost too much to be given up. Therefore, an affectionate father sent at once to his relief a good Samaritan brother, with at least the oil and wine of consolation to the body. Bradwell, a younger brother, who was engaged in that place as a clerk, came and lifted up his aching head, exchanged his rags for a new and comfortable suit, and, as soon as he was restored to health, like the angel sent to Sodom, he persuaded him to flee from that horrible place to some other place of refuge; and Agar says, as he was about to leave, his brother placed in his hand a half crown, saying, at the same time, with a tearful eye,

"I would give thee an hundred pounds, if I thought it would do thee any good."

This, Agar said, went as a dagger to his heart. It was one of those love-taps, gently laid on by the hammer of benevolence, which breaks into pieces the flinty heart. And herein lies the secret and power of the Gospel. The Pharisees could not be made to believe that Christ was to conquer the whole world by human and Divine love. But we see poor Agar now fleeing to another city, sent adrift again on the sea of human depravity and tears, without helm or compass, resolving and re-resolving, a thousand and one times, to dash to the earth the poisonous bowl. But the first sight of a rum-hole, that index to the gates of hell, the first snuff from the bottle of snakes, would sweep, as with a deluge, his resolutions into the gulf of Gehenna, and the almost omnipotent power of habit would bind him with a girdle of brass, and make him a willing slave. Agar says he entered the first tavern he came to, and while negotiating for a drink, his good Samaritan brother, fearing the danger of the seductive trappers by the way, came up on horseback and entered the tavern. Agar says he would not have been more frightened to have seen the devil enter in full uniform, for he knew his presence was a signal of his departure from that pitfall. He then started, and went about two miles farther, to a little village called Merricksville. He entered a tavern, and, without being molested, swallowed one gill of whisky to start with, and soon repeated the dose, and, towards nightfall, he started with two Irish Catholics to go to a tavern, about seven miles distant. When he entered, he found all asleep. He, therefore, stretched himself on the floor, set his bottle by his side, and was again visited by horrible demons; and the landlady said he prayed fervently for mercy, although Agar says he was unconscious of his praying. When the morning came, half crazy and bewildered, a watchful providence led him to the house of a widow Easterns, a Methodist lady. Agar begged of her to shelter him until he could be restored, promising to reward her with any labor she might require at his hands, but she peremptorily refused. But seeing him turn away from her house, there was a still small voice whispered in the widow's ear, saying, "I was a stranger, and ye took me not in." Her heart soon softened, and Agar was called back and comforted with her hospitalities. After some time elapsed, Agar went into the stable belonging to the widow, for the purpose of clearing it. And now, dear reader, prepare your ears to hear a tale, far transcending in horror anything you have thus far listened to. The apostle Paul, in relating his experience, said:

"I knew a man in Christ, above fourteen years ago, whether in the body I cannot tell, or whether out of the body I cannot tell. God knoweth such an one caught up to the third heaven. How he was caught up into Paradise, and heard unspeakable words, which it is not lawful for a man to utter."

But we will now leave the paradistical abode, and descend to the rude stable, made more honorable than the courts of Cæsar, by being the birthplace of Him who is daily colonizing heaven with those who were once publicans, harlots and miserable drunkards. Alas! what do our eyes behold here? A man stretched upon the stable floor? Yes, here lies our friend Agar, with his spirit seemingly departed, and now beholding the reward of a drunkard. But again we are startled. Agar is coming forth from the barn, after a few hours, with his own spirit reanimating his body, and soon he is seated again in the house of the kind widow, perfectly sober and clothed in his right mind. And now we will listen, as we just have to the apostle Paul, although he said it was not lawful for him to relate the particulars seen and heard by his redeemed spirit in the future world. But there was no such prohibition given to the spirit of our friend Agar. His case seemed to be parallel with the apostle Paul, only one had a view of the future and glorious reward of the righteous in paradise, while the other explored the regions and sufferings of the lost. Paul referred back fourteen years to his vision, but Father Hall, as we now call him in Zion, refers back twenty-nine years to his vision in the stable, which, he says, is as familiar as if it were but yesterday, and now, in the fear and love of God, he says he believes his spirit left the body and explored, for some time, the regions of the lost, where it beheld a very great multitude of the most wretched of the sons and daughters of Adam. All seemed to be engaged in hating, taunting and tormenting each other. Whatever prominent and besetting sin controlled them on earth, followed them down to hell, where it was augmented tenfold. Agar clamored, thirsted and panted for whisky, with the burning intensity of a literal flame, while he recognized some of his old acquaintances on earth, and when he was about to grasp the liquor, they cried out,

"Do n't give Agar any, nor old George Lee."

And thus they taunted and tormented him. About this time, there was one stood up in the midst of the hellish throng, and gave out a history of his whole life, in poetry, from his youth until that period. Agar said it was every word true; and, as he gave out that portion of his youth which was a picture of one of the best and kindest of boys, the whole battalion of rowdy fiends would sing the same with a mocking grin, and so on, all the way through his life. Every act of wickedness was related, step after step, in well measured poetry, down to the time he entered their infernal region, which he says was all true. Agar further states that he did not feel to murmur against God in the least, after hearing the song which presented the awful picture of his life. He felt as if he was justly damned. At this point Agar's wrath was inflamed. He declared he would leave for the widow's, and then started upon the run, with every fiend chasing him, and he barely made his escape, as by the skin of his teeth. At this juncture, he felt his spirit reanimating his body, and he awoke to consciousness, and found himself in the stable, which he soon left, as the reader has already been informed, and returned to the comfortable fireside of his hostess. When night came, he proposed to Mrs. E. to go to her brother-in-law's, to lodge that night, about one-fourth of a mile distant, as there were strong men there, who could assist him, if need be, if he should have another fit of deliriums; and, while on his way, Agar said, he saw a man as clear as ever he saw the noonday sun, seemingly about twenty feet high, a mighty giant, proportioned as a man, whose brow seemed to be knit with eternal vengeance, and he said, in tones of thunder:

"My name is Captain Thunderbolt. I dwell betwixt the heavens and the earth, and if you drink any more liquor, I will cut you off from the face of the earth."

Agar said he then begged of him to let him have a little, to wind off with, and he said,

"No, not one drop," and then left him, looking, Agar says, as cross as a bear.

By this time, like Moses, he did exceedingly fear

and quake, not knowing what to do. This character, doubtless, represented the thunderings of the law from Mount Sinai, against all unrighteousness. After this character had passed away, he said, then there appeared before him one of the most lovely persons, who spake unto him in tones of mercy, and told him that he might take little, until he was restored, but after that, he must never take any more. Agar asked him then, how long he would live, should he quit drinking. His kind friend then asked him how many years he had been drinking, to which he answered,

"About seven."

Then Agar asked if he would live as many years if he quit drinking, and he answered,

"Yes, and more too."

He then, with a smile on his face, disappeared.

This last character, doubtless, represented the Gospel, whose office was to bind up the broken-hearted, to heal the wounds of those who had been slain by the law, to seek and save that which was lost.

Agar then went on his journey, and entered the house where he designed to go. His friends then gave him lodgings in a room by himself, but still he was not left alone. Devils and damned spirits, in every horrible shape, he saw, plainly, thronging his room, so that he did not close his eyes in sleep that dreadful night, and when the morning came, he returned to the widow's, who, by the by, was a tavern-keeper. Agar now, when he was about sinking, used his tapering-off license, given to him by his Samaritan friend. Therefore, he took several small drinks that day, to support sinking nature. The second day, he took three drinks, and the third day, which was on the twelfth day of April, 1832, he tapered off on one drink, which, glory be to God, was the last drop of strong liquor that ever wet his lips.

Agar now continued with the widow about two months, during which time his whole wardrobe was not worth a shilling, except his boots. His flesh was bloated, his senses stupefied, and his eye-sight nearly gone; but, he said, he continued to improve every day, as his putrid flesh gave way for that which was natural and healthy, until he shrank down to his usual dimensions. During this time, he would occasionally get upon his knees before God, but it was not long before his praying gave way to swearing; and, after a few months' labor, he got himself comfortably clothed, with a little surplus change, and the following October finds this prodigal lifting the latch of his mother's door, on North St. Paul street, Rochester, safe and sound, gladdening that same heart he had so often lacerated.

Agar now soon engaged himself in a sheepskin tannery, carrying about with him a manly heart, and was again every ounce a man.

CHAPTER TWENTY-SECOND.

But, reader, my pen almost refuses to record what we are compelled to, in order to give you the full-length portrait of this lump of frail humanity. Although he kept his pledge, and ever denied himself strong liquor, but he soon began to dabble in the slop-tubs of beer, wine and cider, and, about New Year, he got in a terrible drunken spree, pouring down the beer. This brought him near to the grave's mouth. He then made a solemn vow that he would never taste of beer again, which vow has been kept inviolate unto this day. The following spring he engaged himself in a stone quarry, at Handford's Landing, where he kept about half boozy on hard cider and wine. Next we find him in a circus at Rochester, where he fell into infamous company. From thence, he said, the old fellow himself seemed to lead him away captive at his will, and about four o'clock in the morning, he entered the house of an aged aunt, that lived about four miles distant from the city, where he soon aroused the inmates, by his blasphemous oaths and filthy conversation, which soon turned that peaceful abode into a bedlam, for whatever place the devil enters is turned into a hell, as, also, the entrance of Christ turns a hell into heaven.

And now, reader, cheer up, for we have come in

sight of the terminus of this filthy, slimy, Bacchanalian route.

At Lima, Livingston county, where he continued some months, digging wells, tending masons, and so forth — but, unfortunately for him, his hard-earned money was sacrificed at the tap of the cider-barrel and the wine cask, all of which was not prohibited at the infancy of the Washingtonian Temperance Society, which was then about starting, a horse-race now, a twin sister to circuses, gambling, and so forth — we find him on a regular cider-burster, as drunk as a fool, and sick as a spoiled oyster. We next find him diving in and crawling out of every rum-hole from Lima to Rochester, and about one o'clock in the morning, on the twentieth day of October, we find this precious lump of humanity stretched on his mother's floor, on North St. Paul street, and when the morning came, he found his whole flesh quivering on his bones, and this cider-fiend threw his whole frame into terrible contortions. Agar said he then, vulture-like, began to snuff for the distant rum-hole, but a kind mother restrained him, and detained him in the house, with a promise to bring him some cider, to which he consented. This was a dreadful day to him, and he only drank when nature was sinking; and this was the day on which he firmly resolved to become a teetotaler, and dash to the devil everything that would intoxicate, redden the eyes, and sting as an adder, except, as in the case of his whisky resolve in Canada, he used his tapering-off license, given to him by his good Samaritan friend. On the twenty-second, he drank a little less, and on the twenty-third — a day never to be forgotten, neither in time or eternity, a day when terror and goodness were joined in their extreme, a day when Agar Hall wet his lips for the last time with the fire-water of dark damnation.

Amen, hallelujah! Glory be to God on high, for a full redemption from the horrible pit of a whisky hell. On this awful and glorious night of the twenty-third, Agar entertained his last surprise party from the regions of woe. He says his room was again thronged with devils ten times more terrific and ferocious than had ever appeared to him before, armed to the teeth with tormenting weapons, as if it was the last grand effort to hold in chains their slave to the lusts of the flesh and servant of Satan. He said he heard them talk and council together, as they held their fatal daggers in their hands. One said:

"I will drive this through his heart, and that will finish him."

He said he then saw a good angel standing at the foot of his bed, with the same smiling, heavenly countenance, like unto the one that came to his relief in Canada, the night he dashed away the strong drink, after Captain Thunderbolt had left him. This friend urged him to pray. Amidst the roarings and hissings of devils, this angelic voice continued to fall, in tones of mercy, on his ear, fervently saying:

"Pray! pray! pray!"

Then, he said, he endeavored to repeat the Lord's prayer, which he had learned in his youth. Agar further states that he was so possessed with the devil, that it was impossible for him to get through with the prayer, as he felt his breath getting shorter and shorter, and he thought, surely, he was dying. He then, with a great effort, leaped from his bed and plunged headlong down a long pair of stairs, and made his way to his mother's bedroom and cried:

"Mother, mother, get a light, for I am dying, I am dying."

His mother spoke unto him roughly, telling him to return to his bed, for there was no danger of his dying. This, he said, broke his heart to pieces, and he began to cry like a little child. Alas! for me, said he, my own dear mother, my last and best friend on earth, has left me. This was not unlike the agony, only in degree of him who cried "my God, my God, why hast thou forsaken me." The mother then arose and lighting a candle, got him some cordial and he returned to bed, and soon he said he thought he was dead and damned; and his spirit again visited the awful pit of woe. He further says, he believes, had any one found him at that time in bed they would have seen a body without a spirit, a lifeless lump of clay.

And now before we explore the infernal regions, we have a word to say to our Universalist friends, bound with us to the eternal world, hopeing and praying they may take warning from the mouth of one that loves their souls.

In the year 1825, Agar says, as he was strolling through the streets of Rochester on the Sabbath day, he discovered the people assembling at a school house near St. Luke's church, and he entered and took his seat and listened to a gray-headed man, preaching Universalist doctrine. The congregation, he said, seemed respectable and intelligent. He also said, he considered himself an ignorant lad, while they, of course, being men and women of age, were of sound judgment. Without looking into the Bible, this simple hearted youth greedily swallowed the seductive poison, so pleasing to the carnal heart.

Ah! says Agar, this is the very doctrine for me. I can now enjoy the pleasure of the theatre and circus, the licentious brothel, rum, rowdyism, and land my soul in heaven at last; and from this anti-hell fire sermon the artless youth was ensnared in this symetrical spider web, and took license, as rumsellers do yearly, to do their work of death according to law, and with his

Universalist license he made his fig leaf apron to conceal his shame, and to serve as a chloroform to stupefy his awakened conscience, from time to time. And now, dear reader, whether you be a Universalist or not, come to the bedchamber of this child of sorrow and tears, and lay your hand on that breast, whose heart still ceases to beat, and if you have tears to weep, let them overflow the banks of your cheeks, while you listen once more to the last report, as seen and heard by the spirit of Agar Hall, of the awful things discovered whilst exploring the regions of the lost. After it returned, and as he thinks, reanimated the second time its own body, which lips and tongue are now reiterating in fair view of the eternal judgment, the things which he clearly saw and heard in moments of sanity, and comparative sobriety, and in the fear and love of God.

Dear reader, whether you believe it or not, he thus relates the following. As he has before stated, he thought he was dead and damned, and in the awful pit of woe, and there beheld great multitudes of both sexes, that would beggar human language to describe their wretchedness and misery. The dove of hope had forever flown, and had given place to the sable winged raven of despair. Many of them had entered through the shiny gate of rum and licentiousness, together with many of the proud nobility of earth, hypocrites and infidels. Agar then cast his eye up to the regions above, where he saw a multitude of the pure and the blessed, very beautifully clad. He said he thought they had once been ministers on earth, and one of them descended with a pair of balances and weighed him, and the scales gave him a little hope. Then, he said, he thought this minister ascended and joined the heavenly multitude, when all ascended still higher and entered the eternal court room of heaven, where he was tried and judged as a criminal on earth. After some time, he said, a little ugly looking old creature, whom he supposed to be the devil, who had been up listening to the trial, now descended, and passing by him went back some distance in the infernal regions, and entered a hole, disappearing from him. And soon came down the heavenly messenger, whose appearance was in glorious contrast with all the prisoners in the pit, and then, with a smile, told Agar he could return to the world, from whence he came, asking him, at the same time, if he ever prayed, to which he answered, that he tried but could not pray in earnest; he then told him he would show him a scene that would create in him a spirit of earnest agonizing prayer, then to-morrow evening, said he, you go to the M. E. Church. He then took him to the place where the devil entered into another apartment which opened into a vast lake, literally flaming with fire, seemingly without shore or bottom, where he beheld thousands of human beings throwing up their arms, floating and flouncing, and strangling as if drowning, all with horrible screechings, crying,

"Oh, Lord Jesus, give us one gill of water."

No language could possibly portray the indescribable horrors his ears listened to and his weeping eyes beheld. Agar said he then was conscious of his spirit again returning and reanimating his body, with his flesh quivering on his bones, as if the earthly tabernacle would be shaken to pieces, and a spirit of fervent prayer to God soon filled the whole region of his soul, and he began to cry aloud, a real Gethsemane agonizing, as if he was determined to take the kingdom of heaven by violence. About eight o'clock in the morning, while on his knees, praying, he said he thought he was surely dying, as his breath continued to grow shorter. He then thought he would call his mother, but at that moment a good spirit whispered in his ear, urging him to hold on to prayer.

"If you die," said the spirit, "die praying."

And soon he found his breath returning, and in a moment the sweet dove of peace gently perched upon his heart, having, in his beak, pardon for the guilty, hope for the despondent, purity for the polluted heart, joy for the disconsolate mourner, and glory, honor, immortality and eternal life crowned and clothed at once this new-born babe in Christ. It was a silent triumph, the green olive-branch of peace. The heart of Agar was then and there changed from nature to grace, and on the twenty-fourth of October, 1823, his name was written in the Lamb's book of life. He then arose from his knees and opened the family bible, with every seal broken by the Lion of the tribe of Judah. He said it appeared to be a new book. All the promises sparkled like so many morning and evening stars. All things about his chamber were tinged with a halo of light. He then went down to the room and told his mother what great things the Lord had done for his soul, and, after warming himself by the fire, he returned to his chamber, where he was met by Apolyon, who made him his prisoner, and locked him up in Doubting Castle until the next Sabbath. Although he went to prayer meetings during the week of his conversion, and immediately after Apolyon turned the key upon him, he cried aloud for the minister or some one to pray with him, and very soon a gray-headed backslider entered the house, and proposed praying for him, and soon they were upon their knees together; and, as he did not seem to draw water from the well of salvation, Agar broke in upon his well-arranged form of prayer, and enquired of him whether he now enjoyed religion, to which the old man replied, he had *once* enjoyed religion, but had lost it.

"Then," said Agar, "if you have n't got it now, there is no use in your praying for me."

And at once the prayer meeting broke up, and so he wandered in dry places, seeking rest and finding none, until Sabbath morning, at half past ten, at the First Methodist church, we find Agar seated in the gallery, in order to listen to a sermon from Father Fillmore. His text was in the first chapter of James, fifth and sixth verses, but he was like the woman that Christ preached to at Jacob's well: he had found a man that exposed, publicly, all the sins of his life. He said he thought Father Fillmore was discharging his whole batteries exclusively at him, and he began to be half offended to think his dreadful character must be exposed before so large an audience of respectable people, but just at that time, his guardian angel came to his relief, and whispered in his ear, saying:

"Agar, this is the Lord Jesus Christ speaking to you by the mouth of Father Fillmore."

And he then believed it; and when the evening sermon was over, a mourner's bench was presented. Agar at once left the gallery, walking the long aisle of the church, and soon fell on his knees at the mercy seat; and amidst the scattered prayers, that seemed to him as random shots, and confusion, old Father Fillmore cried out:

"Try to believe."

From that precious word he grasped again the prize. The day-star of hope arose at once in his heart, amidst chaotic confusion, which was soon succeeded by the full-orbed sun of righteousness, dissipating all his darkness, and shaking to pieces the prison-house of Giant Despair, by the power of free grace, and, like the ancient publican, returned to his mother's house, freely justified, happy in God, commencing with the Holy Spirit. Agar said that was the happiest night of his life, to that period.

CHAPTER TWENTY-THIRD.

Agar says, that during the winter, after his conversion, while laboring in Farmington, he would get blessed while alone, but when in the prayer meetings the cross would be so heavy that he would many times shrink from bearing it, and leave them feeling condemned for not doing something for Jesus, who had done so much for him. And he says, that he used to think he could get along pretty well if it was not for the class-meetings, where he would have to take a part, and in this way he got along, but growing stronger every time he bore the cross. And he said, that he remembered one time, while but a babe in Christ, he attended a Tuesday evening prayer meeting, where there was none of the older brethren to take charge of the meeting, and that they called on him to take the lead. At first he thought he would run and leave them, but something seemed to say to him, What would you have done a few months ago had you gone to one of the rum holes on one of your sprees, and your companions had disappointed you, to which he answered, to himself, that he should have done the best he could to help on the spree; and then thought he would do the best he could there in serving the Lord, so taking the Bible he read the eighteenth Psalm, and he then took the hymn book to read a hymn, and he says that the cross was so heavy that it caused great drops of sweat to fall from his face, but after praying, he felt that he was doubly paid, as it was the best meeting he had ever had.

And on one Monday morning he seemed so tried and buffeted, he says, he thought the enemy of his soul would surely have him, and as he went away by himself for prayer, he felt impressed to go to Father Fillmore, where he thought he could unburden his mind, and that Father Fillmore would tell him just what to do, so that he could go on in the heavenly way, rejoicing. On his way he met a brother, to whom he told his trouble of mind, and whom he was seeking. This brother told him where he would find Father Fillmore, but that he would be much more likely to get help from his class-leader; but Agar, thinking that the minister would know how to help him out of his distress of mind, proceeded to the place where Father Fillmore was, and after telling him how he felt, he asked him what he should do. To this Father Fillmore merely asked him if he ever prayed. To which Agar said, he did pray in secret only. Then Father Fillmore told him he could do nothing for him. He then returned home, feeling very sadly, to think that one who had so lately told him in the sermon, before mentioned, all things that he ever did, and now could not tell him what to do ; but even this, he said, did him good.

Agar says, that in the fall of 1834, while he was working in digging a well a few miles from Rochester, a Presbyterian minister, living in a part of the house where he was staying, was standing by while Agar was digging the well, and asked him if he had found the water which springeth up into everlasting life. Agar thought at first that he would not tell him, but then again he thought that he must not deny his Lord and Master, so he told him that he had tasted of the waters of life. He then told him he was going to have a prayer meeting at his house that night, and wished him to come in and enjoy it with them, to whioh Agar consented, and at this meeting, after two or three had prayed the minister told him to pray, to which he made excuses, saying,

"That he had never prayed in public, since his conversion." (This was before the prayer meeting which we have mentioned.)

But to all of his excuses the minister would not listen, but continued urging him to pray. At length he ventured on that promise which he found verified unto him, "Open thy mouth and I will fill it." And this he found greatly strengthened him.

In the following spring he entered the shop of a brother Hume, in Rochester, who wished him to go to class with him that night. This Agar thought would be a great cross for him, but fearing he would bring on himself darkness and condemnation if he refused, accepted the invitation and went. Upon entering the meeting, which was conducted by the minister in charge, whom they called Father Hibbard, he seemed to tremble as if his limbs would give way, and he thought if he trembled so before as minister of the Lord, what would he do when he came to stand before the Judge of all the earth.

He still had lingering about him the belief that if he could tell some old experienced minister just how he felt, that they could inform what course to pursue, so that the way would be easier for him.

After the meeting was over he tarried to tell this minister some things which had long been on his mind, and also to ask him some questions, and to every thing which Agar asked, or told him, Father Hibbard would say in a kind and loving way, "Look to the Lord."

Which, Agar says, was worth thousands of gold and silver to him, as he thought if that was all the advice such experienced men as Father Hibbard would give him to the Lord, he would go, and he has ever since found him a better counsellor than man. Agar says, that as he followed that good advice of Father Hibbard, that he grew in grace, and the way brighter and better. And a class leader by the name of Father Eggleston would urge him to press on to know the full power of Jesus' blood to cleanse him from all sin, and sanctify him wholly. And about this time Father Hibbard gave him a love feast ticket, with this text,

"For this is the will of God, even your sanctification."

Which, he said, greatly encouraged him, as he believed firmly from that time that that state of grace there spoken of was for him to enjoy, and in the latter part of June he attended a camp meeting, held in Victor, which was the first one he ever had the privilage of attending. He says he went, fully believing, that, although he was then a poor coward in the school of Christ, he would there receive the blessing of perfect love, during the camp meeting. After one of the sermons, the minister said they could have a prayer meeting in the altar. And as Agar was sitting there the tempter told him to go and let some one have the room there, that could pray. He started, thinking he would leave, but somehow, instead of leaving, he soon found himself upon his knees among the other christians, praying earnestly in an audible voice, for the blessings of God to rest upon him. While thus engaged, he says that he began to think that his voice was above all the rest, but he thought, as they had heard him, he might as well keep praying, which he did, and this helped him greatly in overcoming the fear of man.

Thus the meeting increased in interest and in power, until Sabbath morning, when we find Agar sitting back of the tents, by the stove, warming himself, where he began to meditate upon the goodness of God to him, and the spirit of the Lord came upon him in great power, and his heart began to melt under its influence, causing the tears to stream down his cheeks, and something seemed to whisper to him:

"This is the great blessing of holiness, which you have been seeking. Get up and declare it to the people."

Then something seemed to say to him:

"Wait until you are in meeting."

Which, likely, was a temptation from the adversary of his soul. [This was on the twenty-ninth of June, 1835, that Agar says he was sanctified.] But he did not yield, we shall see, for, as the spirit of the Lord urged him to proclaim what he had done for him, he quickly obeyed, and as he arose, and began telling how the Lord had filled him with that perfect love that casts out fear, the people came from all quarters to listen to this story of the dealings of the Lord with his soul; and all through the day, he said, he felt the spirit operating on his heart in such a powerful manner, that he could hardly speak aloud, and in the evening a brother Hayden preached a sermon, which, Agar says, seemed just the one for him, and, so child-like seemed his confidence, that when that minister spoke of his having chosen another subject, but the Lord seemed to hold him to that one, Agar says he thought it was changed on purpose for him.

On Monday morning, as the camp-meeting was about breaking up, Agar says they had a meeting, similar to a love-feast. After the ministers had talked, he improved the first moments given to own his Saviour before the great congregation, and as the Lord began to pour his spirit upon him, he trembled so that he could not stand, and sank upon his knees, perfectly helpless, and held on to a pole which was around the altar, until he felt his strength returning, and his voice came again, and then, springing up, he began again to shout and praise the Lord, for the wonders he had wrought for him. But this hurt the tender ears of some poor, cold-hearted professor standing by, who, taking hold of him, began shaking him, and told him to stop, be quiet; that he wanted to hear what the people said. But an inward voice seemed to whisper to Agar:

"Quench not the spirit."

After this meeting closed, Agar started for his home at Rochester, rejoicing in the love of God; and while on the way, he says, he heard a person swearing, and he says that oaths never sounded to him so vile as they did then. He left his home in Rochester, in a few days, for Caledonia, where he had been working before camp-meeting, and where he was now going to find more employment. While on his way there, his heart was so filled with the love of Jesus, that he would stop at the houses on the way, to tell what a Saviour he had found, and pray with them, and he was so lost and swallowed up in doing the will of his Heavenly Father, that when he had arrived at his destination, he could not realize how he got there. Agar says he stayed there two or three months, and then was in different places, laboring, and remembering all the while to keep, faithfully, the vows he had made to God, at the camp-meeting before mentioned, doing every known duty, and owning what the Lord had done for him, at every opportunity. The Lord was with him, and he continued to rejoice in the Rock of his salvation; and Agar says, one time, while working in Caledonia, a brother B——, the minister, told him that if he could not pray differently, he had better not pray at all. This, he says, almost killed him, as he was young in his experience then. He thought that he must obey him. So he would attend meetings, but dare not pray; and then he would go away, feeling condemned, until he felt so bad he could neither eat nor sleep. So he left there and went back to Rochester, and found that Father Fillmore was holding a protracted meeting, which he attended, but still did not feel as though he could speak or pray. At length, finding he could not get along, he arose in a meeting and told just how he felt, what the minister at Caledonia had told him, and how he had been afraid to take part in the meetings; and in doing this, he says he seemed to gain a victory. Then the pastor of the church where Agar belonged told him he must not mind anything about such orders, but obey King Jesus in all things, and encouraged him to be faithful in the discharge of his duty, which advice he took, and was again on his way rejoicing. Thus Agar began soon to find these words of our Saviour applicable to him:

"The servant is not greater than his Lord. If they have persecuted me, they will also persecute you."

At another time, in Rochester, as there was a protracted meeting there in progress, two brethren went away some distance, and persuaded a Professor M—— to come to Rochester to assist in the meetings, and Agar says the first night he attended the meetings, he went into the altar, with the brethren, to pray, and seemed to be led to pray for the church. After a season of prayer, this Professor M. said he wished them to pray expressly for sinners. This, Agar says, he thinks was all right, as there were some there whom they had called forward to pray for. But the next night he thought that he would let them do the praying in the altar without him, and so he knelt at the outside of the altar, where he commenced praying, and the Lord blessed him, so that he soon praised him, David-like, before the whole congregation, when this Professor M. approached him, and told him to stop. But Agar had begun to learn that it was better to obey God than man. After repeating his orders several times, he then told Agar that he was making all the people laugh. Agar answered: "Let them laugh on They will cry in hell unless they repent."

The professor repeated his commands to Agar to stop, to which Agar replied, that if he should stop the very stones would cry out.

After the meeting closed, Agar says he returned home praising God, and never spent a happier night; feeling so much of the presence of the Lord, that he could not sleep.

One winter in Rochester, Agar says, as he and a good old Father Stuart was visiting from house to house, holding prayer meetings, and talking and praying with sinners; and the Lord was owning their labors by blessing them and the people, leading souls to himself; when one afternoon, as they were about passing St. John's church, where they belonged, and as they saw the people gathering there, they went in, and on finding they were having a meeting, they took their seats and remained there. A brother B—— was the preacher on that charge, but a brother T—— had the charge of the meeting, who, after making a very long prayer and exhortation, said that they would let the sisters occupy the time, as they had not had as much opportunity for taking part in the meeting as the brethren; then as some of them were speaking, this very same brother T——, who had occupied so much time himself, would keep crying out, "be short, be short," until they were all afraid to speak, and the time was running to waste, Agar arose and told them that he had many times felt hurt, by some praying and talking long enough to preach a short sermon, and then telling them to "be short;" that if he had always obeyed those in high authority, he might have then been in the bottomless pit, instead of being there, happy in God. On hearing this, brother B——, the minister, thought he must mean him, and jumping up told the people that he had tried to persuade Agar to do differently about some things, but that as he *would not*, he did not know what he could do with him, and as Agar had no reference to this minister, but the one at Caledonia, he again arose to tell him he did not mean him, when the one who was taking the leading of the meeting, arose also to have him stop and listen to the ministers.

Upon that, Agar told him, the brother T——, that if he had any advice to give, to give it to his wicked boys at home, and as the minister was still talking, Agar said:

" Brother B——, you are made of no better flesh and blood than I am, if you do wear better clothes."

At this criiss the minister came and opening the door, told Agar he must leave; when Agar says he felt as though he would like to pray for him, and asked him if he might, but the minister not seeming at all willing, he emerged into the storm, for it was a very stormy day, rejoicing in God, not yet seeing that he had done anothing wrong.

A few days after this the minister met Agar in the street, and saluted him by asking him when he would be ready for trial. Which, by the way was the first intimation Agar had *had* of a trial, but nevertheless told him he was ready any time. Then in a few days one of the official members accosted him in the street and read to him a long list of charges, and told him on Friday afternoon he must go to the church for trial. He was persuaded by some of his friends to get a local preacher to go as his council, and see that he was dealt with fairly. When they arrived there on Friday, he says, brother B—— was sitting there as accuser, and judge and five of the official members for jurymen, and a great many others for witnesses against him. After praying, they proceeded with the witnesses, who testified so many things against him that he says he sometimes thought they would bring up things which he did while a poor drunkard—they seemed so bent on having him expelled. After the examining of the witnesses was finished the jurymen left the room a short time, and on returning said, they had cleared him of all the charges except his talking saucy to the minister; and thought he had better confess to brother B——, and then it would all be right again; but as Agar did not yet see that he had done anything out of the way, he says that he thought that to ask their forgiveness would be like asking a priest to forgive his sins, and he would not do it. And they were just about to expel him, when one of the class leaders proposed their letting him have a week to consider upon it, to which they agreed, and so let it rest.

And the next day as one of his brethren was talking with him, the light of God's spirit shone upon his mind, and he felt sorrry for what he had said, and was willing, and resolved to confess it as soon as he could have an opportunity.

The Sabbath following, he says, he believes that the sermon was a message from God to him, which was preached from the text found in the seventh chapter of second Corinthians, tenth verse, which is:

" For Godly sorrow worketh repentance to salvation, not to be repented of, but the sorrow of the world worketh death."

And on Monday evening, as soon as there was a chance given in the meeting for speaking, Agar improved it in fulfilling his resolution, so he arose and told them that he had felt very bad about being expelled from the church, so that his sleep had fled from him several nights, but that the spirit of the Lord had shone upon his heart, and he now asked the forgiveness of all that he had in any way injured; and that it would have taken a strong rope a few days before to have held him, but now he was so humbled that they could lead him by a thread. And then brother B—— took him by the hand and said to him, you are restored to the church. And he says this trial was worth more to him than all the money in the bank of England; and this proved to be the first and last trial he has ever had.

Agar's father and mother, and three brothers and two sisters are all gone to the spirit world, and he is left a lonely pilgrim, traveling around to camp-meetings and quarterly meetings, trying to lead poor sinners to the Lamb of God, which taketh away the sins of the world, by telling how the Lord has so wonderfully rescued him from the horrible pit and miry clay, and hid him in the rock of ages; where, he says, he feels that he is now hid, and his soul is filled with the love of God, and he knows if he should leave this world he would go right home to glory.

There, reader, you have read the unvarnished, simple-hearted, child-like story, as if told while sitting around the domestic hearth, just as the thing happened, not very gramatical or rhetorical. Whoever has read the life of John Bunyan, the greatest author of this world, (save the inspired writers) will find it served up in about the same kind of homespun style; and the author, brought up by grace from about as low a pit as was Agar, and raised to the honorable cognomen of the friend of Jesus. Twelve years in Bedford jail for rebuking the popular sins of the day, was to John Bunyan what Agar's sore trial was while insisting that even a minister in charge was made of no better flesh and blood than he was, although wearing finer and more fashionable cut clothes. But now, without further comment, Tell Tale Rag must give the parting hand to the reader, and commence the second volume of this work, and search for the popular sins of our other six masters.

You will next hear from me at Scavenger's Ally, Rag Bag Hall, which place I was gathered in, with many of my companions in tribulation, from the gutters of the streets, after serving faithfully my six masters.

www.ingramcontent.com/pod-product-compliance
Lightning Source LLC
LaVergne TN
LVHW010242110826
845151LV00004B/1372

* 9 7 8 1 4 2 5 5 2 4 0 1 2 *